FROM THE MOVIE

Disney

WISH

THE MOVIE NOVELISATION

Adapted by Erin Falligant

SCHOLASTIC
SYDNEY AUCKLAND NEW YORK TORONTO LONDON MEXICO CITY
NEW DELHI HONG KONG BUENOS AIRES PUERTO RICO

Disney

WISH

Published by Scholastic Australia in 2023.

Scholastic Australia Pty Limited
PO Box 579 Gosford NSW 2250
ABN 11 000 614 577
www.scholastic.com.au

Part of the Scholastic Group
Sydney • Auckland • New York • Toronto • London • Mexico City
New Delhi • Hong Kong • Buenos Aires • Puerto Rico

ISBN 978-1-76026-492-5

Printed in Australia.

FSC
www.fsc.org
MIX
Paper from responsible sources
FSC® C001695

The paper in this book is FSC® certified.
FSC® promotes environmentally responsible, socially beneficial and economically viable management of the world's forests.

Scholastic Australia's policy, in association with its printers, is to use papers that are renewable and made efficiently from wood grown in responsibly managed forests, so as to minimise its environmental footprint.

Chapter One

In a cozy cottage nestled in the forest, seventeen-year-old Asha helped her grandfather with his cape. As she fastened buttons, she told the story of Rosas, the beautiful city they called home.

"Once upon a time," Asha began, "on a faraway island stood a most magical kingdom, founded by a most magical king with the power to grant wishes. People settled there from far and wide in the hopes that their dreams may come true."

Asha had seen King Magnifico grant many wishes—one each month in a special wish ceremony. But today, Asha thought of only one wish and one wisher: her grandfather, Saba Sabino.

She finished the story with a flourish. "But everyone agrees there is none more deserving than . . . my grandfather, a most glorious, loving, handsome man who turns one hundred years old today!"

Behind them, a little goat wearing yellow pajamas scampered onto a shelf, but Asha barely noticed as she finished buttoning her saba's cape. Then she held up a mirror.

Sabino smiled at his reflection, his eyes twinkling beneath bushy white eyebrows that matched the tufts of hair on his head. "And I still have my favorite teeth," he said.

Asha laughed as she packed up her pouch, tucking her favorite sketchbook inside. "It can't be a coincidence the king called a wish ceremony today of all days," she said. She knew Saba Sabino longed to have his wish granted.

Sabino rapped his knuckles against his head for good luck. "Oh, jinx, jinx," he said, "everyone stinks."

"Don't be like that, Saba," said Asha. "Tonight's your night. I can feel it." She kissed his cheek.

"Well, you know what they say," said Saba. "Anything is possible . . ."

Just then, Asha's mother, Sakina, stepped into the room carrying a basket of yarn.

"In the Kingdom of Wishes!" Sakina, Asha, and Saba finished together.

Sakina laughed, her dark curls tucked beneath a magenta headscarf. Then she glanced around the room. "Where's Valentino?"

Asha and Sabino started to search the shelves above

just as Valentino toppled from his perch into Sakina's basket. "Got him," said Sakina.

Asha reached for Valentino, who bleated in protest. "Sorry, I don't speak goat," she said as she placed him gently on the floor. Valentino immediately climbed back up onto the fireplace mantle.

"Let's start on Saba's cake," Sakina suggested.

"Oh, I can't," Asha said quickly. "I'm giving a tour." She had a special job in Rosas. When tourists arrived at the harbor, Asha greeted the visitors and guided them around the kingdom.

"And then . . . um. I'm—I'm helping Dahlia," Asha stammered, letting her dark braids spill over her face so she wouldn't have to look her mother in the eye. Asha was going to the castle where her best friend worked, but not to help her. Asha had a secret meeting that she couldn't tell her family about—at least not yet. "Yeah, so . . ."

"Why'd you say it like that?" asked her mother. She put a hand on her hip.

"Like what?" said Asha innocently.

"What are you up to?" asked Sakina, pointing a knowing finger at Asha.

Asha shrugged. "What makes you think that I'm up to something?"

"Because I know your pauses," said Sakina.

"I'm maturing," said Asha. "My pauses are changing." She gave her mom a quick kiss.

"Asha—" said Sakina.

"Can't talk now," said Asha. "I'm gonna be late." As she rushed out the door, she called over her shoulder, "I'll see you at the wish ceremony!"

Asha raced down the hill toward the kingdom, with Valentino scampering close behind. In the harbor, a ship had docked. Tourists were already spilling onto the pier.

Asha rushed past the WELCOME TO ROSAS! sign. "I'm here, I'm here, I'm here," she said, panting. "Just one second. Let me catch my breath." Then she greeted the tourists in several languages to be sure they all felt welcome. "¡Hola! Shalom! Salam! Everyone ready?"

Asha led the group through a grand arch. As they walked up the main road, they passed joyful bakers, florists, and musicians. Valentino leaped onto a stone wall for a better view.

The wide-eyed tourists took in all the lucky townspeople who'd had their wishes granted by King Magnifico. *Any* wish could be granted, Asha explained, whether it was to be a talented dancer, to have long, luxurious hair, or to travel to outer space.

Asha paused to show off the incredible fruits and flowers grown in Rosas, the result of wishes come true. Then she opened the ornate gates that led into the bustling marketplace.

The tourists marveled at the beautiful castle and the banners adorned with images of the handsome king. Asha told the visitors that King Magnifico had founded the city of Rosas many years ago. The king was a generous and powerful sorcerer, she added.

"And someone that I'd like to kiss," murmured one of the tourists, who swooned at a statue of the handsome king.

"Oh dear," said Asha.

She redirected the tourists' attention to a puppet show, which told how wishes were given and granted: When citizens of Rosas turned eighteen, they handed over their wish to the king in a special ceremony.

"Does it hurt?" asked a tourist.

"Do you cry?" asked another.

Asha assured the tourists that wish giving was a painless process. A person who gave the king their wish wouldn't miss it. In fact, they wouldn't even remember what they had wished for! But they could be confident that the king would keep their wish safe. And then, once a month, the king granted the wish of one lucky citizen.

Asha led the tourists toward a bridge that overlooked the harbor. As they stopped to admire the view, Asha explained that in Rosas, anything was possible. Although she hadn't given her wish to the king yet, she knew that *no* wish was off-limits.

Asha cued Valentino for the grand finale. The little goat kicked a lever with his back hoof, causing a carpet to roll down the steps and spraying confetti into the air.

Each and every tourist got caught up in the celebration. "I want to live here!" announced a tall man.

"Do you really forget your wish once you give it?" asked a mother traveling with her daughter.

"You forget without regret!" Asha answered. "As the saying goes."

"I'll give my wish!" cried the young daughter, waving her hand in the air.

"I want to meet the king!" added the woman who had fainted at the mere sight of his statue moments ago.

"You're in luck," said Asha. "There's a wish ceremony tonight! You're welcome to stay and watch. Now, who's hungry?"

Right on cue, servers arrived and laid out an inviting spread of breads, fruits, meats, and desserts. "Compliments of Chef Mariana," Asha explained, "who got her wish to be the greatest chef in the world!"

"Oh, this is delicious!" declared a tourist.

As the tourists surrounded the food, Asha took the opportunity to step away. "Enjoy!" she called as she hurried toward the castle.

It was almost time for Asha's secret meeting. And this time, she couldn't be late.

Chapter Two

Asha hurried into the castle kitchen with Valentino close at her heels. There, shelves were stocked with breads and beautifully decorated cakes. Dahlia, in a crisp red apron and wire-rimmed glasses, was mixing batter behind the counter. At just sixteen years old, she was already a master baker.

"Hello. Hi. Help me, best friend and honorary doctor of all things rational," said Asha, relieved to see Dahlia. "My interview is in one hour. I'm so nervous I could explode." As if to make her point, Asha ran circles around the counter.

This was the secret meeting Asha had kept from her family. Today, she was interviewing to be the king's apprentice. She was so nervous!

"Interview?" said Dahlia, who was now mixing herbs in a mug. "What interview?"

"Dahlia!" Asha exclaimed. How could her best friend joke at a time like this?

"Ooh, you mean the interview with our velvety sweet buttercream of a king," said Dahlia with a lovesick smile.

"Please don't say it like that," said Asha.

"My best friend, the king's apprentice," Dahlia crooned. "I'll be famous."

"I've forgotten how to talk," said Asha. "I have no words. Is my mouth drooping?" She tugged at the corners of her mouth.

"Only when you pull it," said Dahlia. "Drink this. It's rose and lavender. Good for nerves." She offered Asha the mug.

Asha sipped the tea, her eyes wide. "Quick," she said, "ask me an interview question."

"Okay," said Dahlia thoughtfully. "What's your weakness?"

"Weakness?" said Asha. "Uh, I get irrational when I'm nervous."

"No, no," said Dahlia, correcting her. "You care too much."

"I do?" said Asha. "Is that a weakness?"

"That's why it's perfect," said Dahlia, proud of the answer she'd proposed. "You're welcome."

"Oh, I think I'm going to be sick," said Asha.

Dahlia quickly slid the bowl of batter away from

Asha. "This is a kitchen, don't even joke," said Dahlia. "Just relax. You're surrounded by friends."

I am? thought Asha. She glanced around the room.

Dahlia gave a sly grin and lifted the cloth from a tray of warm cookies that were decorated to look like the handsome king. The smell wafted toward Simon, who was snoozing on a sack of flour in the corner. "Mmm, cookies?" he asked, yawning. Eighteen-year-old Simon was a gentle ginger-haired giant who always seemed in need of a nap.

Moments later, four other teens raced toward the counter, lured by the smell of Dahlia's baking. Hal, Safi, and Gabo jockeyed for position, their eyes on the prize.

"Cookies."

"Look out!"

"Mine."

"Cookies!" Dario echoed. But unlike the other teens, the tall, lanky blond ran right past the counter and out of the kitchen. The others watched him go, then shrugged.

Thirteen-year-old Gabo, who was shorter than the rest, had to fight to reach a cookie.

"Careful, Safi!" Dahlia warned a curly-haired teen. "They're lemon—"

Safi, who was allergic to almost everything, suddenly sneezed all over the tray of cookies.

Gabo yanked his hand back. "No!" he groaned. "Ah. Life is so unfair!"

"You can have mine, Gabo," someone offered sweetly.

Gabo whirled around to find Bazeema, a slender teen in a yellow dress who seemed to have appeared out of nowhere. "Bazeema! Argh!" cried Gabo. "Where'd you come from?"

The shy teen had a habit of sneaking up on her friends and disappearing just as quickly. She smiled. "I've been here the whole time."

Gabo took the cookie and bit off the head. "Ew, gross!" he said, spitting it out. "Are these healthy?"

"Of course," said Dahlia. "That's how the king likes them."

"Oh, there go my nerves again," said Asha at the mention of the king. She gulped the tea, hoping the herbs would calm her down.

"Oh, right," Gabo responded. "Your interview with the king. Don't worry. We'll be here for you when you fail."

"Gabo!" Hal exclaimed. With her infectious smile and shiny hoop earrings, Hal was every bit as sunny as Gabo was grumpy.

"What?" Gabo said. "Most people fail at everything."

Just then, Dario returned to the kitchen. "Oh, *there* are the cookies!" he said, reaching for one.

"Dario, look out!" Dahlia warned. "Safi sneezed on those."

"Oh," said Dario. "Okay, cool. Thanks." Then he promptly took a bite.

Gabo shuddered at the sight. "Anyway," he said, turning back toward Asha, "not that I blame you for trying to cheat the system."

Asha raised an eyebrow. "What?" she said. "I'm not trying to cheat anything."

"Come on," Gabo countered. "Everyone knows that the king's apprentices get their wishes granted and usually their family's wishes, too."

Asha opened her mouth to argue, but Gabo wasn't wrong exactly. She did hope the king would grant Saba's wish.

"Not always," said Dahlia, jumping to Asha's defense. She tried to name an apprentice who hadn't had their wish granted, but she couldn't think of one. "Well, maybe always."

"Your saba's a hundred today and still waiting," Gabo pointed out.

The other teens rallied around Asha, offering support:

"Tonight's his night."

"I can feel it."

"Everybody thinks so."

"Ignore him."

But Gabo went on. "Not to mention the fact that you're also turning eighteen—"

"Happy birthday!" Dario blurted to Asha.

"In a few months," Gabo continued. "And when you give your wish to the king, you don't want to have to end up like Simon here."

From his cozy flour-sack bed, Simon's eyes popped open. "What's wrong with Simon here?" he asked sleepily.

"It's not your fault," said Gabo dismissively. "Everyone becomes boring after they give their wish."

Simon sat straight up. "Have I become boring?" he asked, sounding hurt. "Do you all think that?"

As if to change the subject, Safi suddenly sneezed.

"Not boring," said Asha quickly. "No, just—"

"More peaceful," Hal pointed out.

"Calmer," Dahlia added.

"More . . . content?" Bazeema offered.

Simon's face sunk. He knew his friends were only being nice.

"Simon, don't worry," said Asha. "You're still you, and I bet you get your wish granted really soon."

"Unlike your poor old saba," grumbled Gabo, "who's still waiting."

Asha, who had heard enough from him, scooped up a handful of flour and blew it in Gabo's face.

"Asha?" someone called from nearby.

Queen Amaya had just entered the room. In her elegant off-white gown and shimmering cape, she looked out of place in the flour-dusted kitchen.

"The queen," Asha murmured under her breath.

The teens scrambled to greet her.

"Oh my goodness," said Dahlia, urging her friends to fall in line. "Quickly."

"This is so exciting," Hal added.

"Don't sneeze," Safi whispered to himself. "Don't sneeze!"

Gabo groaned as he watched the teens scramble. "We're so embarrassing," he muttered.

But every teenager rushed forward to bow or curtsy. Even Valentino dipped his head in respect.

"Cookie?" asked Dario, offering the queen one of the sneezed-upon cookies. Dahlia quickly reached out to lower his hand.

"No, thank you." The queen was all business, ready to find the king's next apprentice. "Asha, the king is ready for you."

"Now?" said Asha, confused. "Am I late? I thought I—"

"You're fine," the queen assured her. "The last interview—"

From the staircase behind the queen, someone let out a pitiful sob. "It was a disaster!" a man cried as he raced out of the castle.

"Finished early," Amaya concluded. "Shall we?" She turned toward the door.

"Oh, okay," said Asha. "I'm ready!" But her eyes flashed with panic. "I am so *not* ready," she whispered to Dahlia.

"You're fine," Dahlia whispered back. "Just don't touch anything, don't forget to curtsy, and tell him I love him." She paused. "I'm kidding. Do *not* tell him that."

Asha could only nod, wide-eyed, as she followed the queen from the kitchen.

"Bye. Don't get your hopes up," Gabo called after her.

Dahlia didn't have to scold him. Valentino, always loyal to Asha, did it for her. "Baaa!"

Chapter Three

As Asha nervously followed Queen Amaya up a grand staircase, she took in the beautiful surroundings. The staircase curved upward in a seemingly never-ending arc. The mirrors lining the staircase reflected the wonder in Asha's face.

The queen offered Asha some advice as they slowly made their way to the top. "The apprentice should always keep the fire going, because the king likes his tea hot," the queen said.

"Uh-huh," said Asha, listening carefully.

"He also likes to talk, quite a bit," added the queen with a laugh. "Feel free to just listen."

"Oh, I'm a good listener," said Asha brightly. With each step, she felt a bit less nervous. The queen had an unexpected way of putting her at ease.

"He's very particular," Queen Amaya continued. "Everything has its place."

"Oh," said Asha with a hint of curiosity.

"Some items might seem strange, but why a sorcerer needs what a sorcerer needs is not your concern," the queen reminded her.

"Right," Asha agreed.

"And above all, do not expect to see the wishes," warned Queen Amaya. "Don't even ask."

"Yes, ma'am," said Asha. "I mean, I won't, Your Majesty."

Much too soon, they reached the tall doors to King Magnifico's study. Amaya turned toward Asha and said, "I'm rooting for you, Asha."

"You are?" said Asha. She hadn't realized the queen knew her!

"Mm-hmm," said the queen.

"Thank you, ma'am," said Asha. She stroked one of her braids and asked softly, "But . . . why?"

"I see the way you look out for others," explained Queen Amaya, gazing straight into Asha's eyes. "It's clear how much you love this kingdom and its people."

"Well, of course," said Asha, her cheeks flushing.

"That kind of generosity has always been the true essence of Rosas," said the queen.

"Huh," said Asha with a nervous laugh. She glanced away, pleased and humbled by the compliment.

Amaya took Asha's hands in hers. "Now," she said warmly, "are you ready to meet the king?"

"Oh, I hope so," murmured Asha. She took a deep breath, bracing herself as Amaya pushed open the heavy doors to King Magnifico's study.

"Wow," Asha murmured. She stepped into a large circular room with an ornately tiled floor and bookshelves stretching toward the ceiling. Rolled-up scrolls rested on a majestic desk. Herbs, flowers, and even animal organs floated in glass jars. But King Magnifico was nowhere to be seen.

"He'll be right with you," Queen Amaya assured Asha. "I'm going to check on the ceremony."

"Oh, okay," said Asha, surprised that the queen would leave her here alone. "Um . . . bye."

As the queen stepped out, Asha caught her own reflection in a large mirror. Even in her most grown-up lavender dress, she looked just as small and overwhelmed as she felt.

Then her attention drifted to the books. She stepped toward the shelves and read the titles printed along the spines: "*Fire Magic . . . History of Spells . . .*"

One book was locked in a glass case decorated with etchings. "Oh wow," Asha murmured as she examined them. They were winged insects—hornets. "Hmm . . ." She reached out to touch one.

"No, no," boomed a voice behind her. "No, no, no. Asha, that book is forbidden."

Asha turned to see King Magnifico standing before

the mirror. When he stepped into the light, it illuminated his handsome features—piercing blue eyes, perfectly swooped silver hair, and an angled jaw beneath a closely shaved beard.

"Oh!" Asha said, startled. "Hi. I was just, umm . . ." When she pointed toward the etchings on the glass case, they suddenly came to life. The buzzing insects darted at her like real hornets!

"Ah! What's happening?" Asha cried. "Get away from me!" She waved her arms wildly.

The king rushed to help her. "I—I put a spell on the glass!" he explained.

"I just thought the etchings were pretty!" said Asha, ducking to avoid the swarm.

"Yes, but the book—the book is dangerous," said the king.

Asha spun this way and that, dodging the hornets. "Then why have it?" she managed to ask.

"A king must be prepared for everything," he explained. "Hold on. Don't move. I got it." As he gestured with his hands, the hornets began flying obediently back toward the glass case.

"Are they deadly?" Asha asked. "They seem deadly!" She still flailed wildly.

"Please. No. Oh, hold still," the king begged her. "Hold still."

"No—get away!" Asha cried. "Get away! Shoo! Shoo! Shoo! Shoo!" She spun side to side, batting at the air. But when she realized the hornets were gone, she paused to catch her breath.

"A bit of exercise," said the king, amused. "Um, are you okay?"

"No!" she blurted. "I mean—yes." Had she blown her chance for the apprenticeship? She gave an awkward curtsy. "And I understand if you want me to leave and never show my face again."

"Oh, please, let's not overreact," said the king. "You're here. You've certainly got my attention. So, Asha, go ahead. Tell me why you think you should be my apprentice," he said as he went behind his desk.

"Okay, well . . ." Asha tried to remember Dahlia's advice. "I care too much."

"Okay . . . ," said the king hesitantly. "That's interesting."

"It's my weakness," Asha explained, clasping her hands. "Figured I might as well get through all the bad stuff right up front."

The king smiled. "Fair enough," he said. "And your strengths?"

"Glad you asked," said Asha brightly. Her words came out in a rush. "I'm a quick learner and a hard worker. And I help well. And I'm young, so I'm malleable—but not too young so that I'm too malleable! And I'm always on time. Oh, and I like to draw. Is this anything?"

She pulled out her journal and flipped the pages with her thumb. The doodles of Valentino she had drawn in the corner of each page came to life, making it appear as if he were jumping.

"Uh . . . what am I looking at?" asked the king, squinting.

"It's a goat," said Asha, flipping the pages again.

"Oh!" said the king.

"It's hopping," she explained.

"Certainly," said the king, raising his eyebrows.

"See?" said Asha, giving the pages another flip.

"Oh! Again," murmured the king.

"It's, uh, hopping," Asha whispered self-consciously.

"That is a unique . . . talent?" the king finally said. "Do we call that a talent?"

When Asha realized that the king was only being polite, she lowered her journal. "It's just something my father taught me." She gave a small, sad smile.

The king saw the longing on her face. "I remember your father," he said gently.

"Really?" said Asha.

"He was quite the philosopher and dreamer," said the king. "I used to love talking to him about the stars."

Asha smiled and flipped to another a drawing in her

journal. Her sketch showed Asha sitting with her father in the wishing tree. "We used to climb that tree on the high ridge where it becomes just you and the stars," she told the king. "He'd say the stars are there to guide us, to inspire us, to remind us to believe in possibility. Even when he was sick, he'd take me out at night to dream. All I dreamed about was him getting better."

The king nodded with understanding. "How old were you when he passed?"

"Twelve," said Asha.

"It's not fair, is it?" the king said kindly.

Asha shook her head.

"When I was young, I too suffered great loss," offered the king.

"I didn't know that," said Asha. "I'm sorry."

The king gazed toward a tattered, burned tapestry on the wall. "My entire family, our lands were destroyed by selfish, greedy thieves," he explained. "If only I'd known magic then. . . ." He gazed at the tapestry. "This is all that remains. Well, this and me, I suppose."

He turned to face Asha again. "You see, I founded this kingdom so there would be a place where everyone is safe. Asha, no one should ever have to see their dreams destroyed before their eyes."

Asha couldn't have agreed more. "No one should have to live their life feeling the pain of that loss every day," she said.

"And that's why I do what I do," said the king.

"And that's why I want to work for you," said Asha simply.

King Magnifico nodded thoughtfully, impressed by her conviction. Then he made his decision. "Come with me," he said, gesturing toward tall mirrors. With a wave of his hand, the mirrors opened into a wide doorway.

If Asha was to be his new apprentice, then he would need to show her the wonders that lay just beyond those doors. . . .

CHAPTER FOUR

King Magnifico led Asha into a large round chamber with tall windows and a star-shaped pattern on the tile floor. "You're one of the very few I've ever invited in here," he said. "But if I'm to trust you, I need to know you understand just how important they are."

"They?" Asha asked. She looked up and gasped. A sea of glowing bubbles floated beneath the domed ceiling.

"The wishes of Rosas," the king said solemnly.

Asha clutched her chest, overwhelmed by a feeling of joy and love.

"You can feel them already, can't you?" said the king with a delighted smile. "Careful—they're exhilarating."

He led Asha toward the center of the room. When he waved his arms, the wish bubbles descended and swirled around him. The glowing, grapefruit-sized bubbles were cloudy, but when Magnifico swirled his hand around a group of wishes, the cloudiness cleared. Now, visible within each bubble was an animated scene of the wisher's most joyous wish.

"Hello, my dear friends," said the king. "How are you?"

The images of the people inside the wishes smiled and waved at Magnifico.

"They're so . . . alive," Asha whispered. In response, the people turned toward Asha, examining her with curious, concerned faces. "And now they're looking at me?"

"It's okay," Magnifico said soothingly to the wishes. "I invited her. You know I would never do anything to put you at risk."

As the wish bubbles swirled lovingly around Magnifico, he smiled, like a father wrapped in his children's hug. "You see," he said to Asha, "people think wishes are just ideas. But they are part of your heart. The very best part." He gazed back at the precious wishes. "Aren't you?"

As the king cradled the wishes in his hands, Asha could see that he was devoted to protecting them at all costs. Then a few bubbles floated tentatively toward Asha. She recognized the townspeople inside. One man wished to be a mountain climber. He was proudly scaling a mountain peak. A woman whom Asha had seen feeding birds in the courtyard was now flying among them. "Wow . . . ," Asha murmured at the sight.

Magnifico sent the wish bubbles swirling into beautiful, intricate patterns. They formed a long, inviting tunnel and then a rushing stream overhead. As Asha watched in wonder, the patterns kept changing.

Suddenly, she spotted the wish of an elderly man holding a stringed instrument called a lute. It was Saba Sabino! Asha followed the wish through the cloud of swirling bubbles. Finally, she reached Saba's wish.

As it settled gently into her palms, Saba gave her a loving smile from inside the bubble. Asha caught her breath. She felt now what the king must be feeling—that she would protect Saba's wish, no matter what.

King Magnifico was still distracted by the other wishes. "You know," he said, "I'd love to see someone wish to be the best apprentice a mighty sorcerer has ever had. What do you say?" When Asha didn't respond, he turned to see wishes encircling her in adoration. "Well, I'd say the wishes approve." Then the king saw Sabino's wish bubble in Asha's hands.

"It's . . . it's my saba Sabino's wish," Asha explained, blinking back tears. "He looks so joyful." She paused. "You know, it's his birthday today. He's one hundred years old."

"That's impressive," said the king.

"Your Majesty," said Asha, her chest swelling with

hope, "would you maybe consider granting his wish tonight?"

Magnifico watched her balance awkwardly in a curtsy. When he finally spoke, his voice was heavy with disappointment. "Well, that was fast, wasn't it?" he said. "You know most people wait a few months, even a year before they start asking me for things."

"I'm so sorry," Asha said quickly. "I did not mean to—"

"No, it's okay. It's okay," the king interrupted, his voice softening. "Here, let me see the wish."

When she handed it to him, King Magnifico studied Sabino and his lute. "It is a beautiful wish," he said in acknowledgment. "But, unfortunately, it's too dangerous."

"Dangerous?" repeated Asha, confused.

"Your saba longs to create something to inspire the next generation," said the king. "Great wish, but too vague. Create what? A weapon, perhaps? To inspire them to do what? Destroy Rosas, maybe?"

Asha spoke quickly. "My saba would never do anything to hurt anyone."

"You think that—" began the king.

"I know that," Asha said, correcting him.

The king drew back, surprised by her tone. With a wave of his hand, he sent Sabino's wish overhead to join the others.

"Well, you're young," said the king dismissively. "You're young. You don't know anything, really. Whereas, it is my responsibility to only grant the wishes I'm sure are good for Rosas." Without another word, he crossed the room toward his altar and began mixing potions that sparked with magic.

Asha's heart hurt as she watched the wishes floating above. "So . . . most of these wishes will *never* be granted?" she asked.

"Yet I still protect them like all the others," said Magnifico, his gaze fixed on the tubes and beakers of fizzing liquids.

"Can't you just give them back instead?" asked Asha.

"Excuse me?" said the king.

"The wishes," said Asha, her voice rising. "The wishes you're not going to grant. Can't you give them back so those people can at least try to pursue them themselves? You know, if they're dangerous, then they can be stopped, but if they're not—"

"You've completely missed the point," argued the king, his irritation growing. "People come here because they know they can't make their own dreams come true. The journey is too hard. It is too unfair." He reached toward a pool of potion and gathered the glowing magic into his palms before continuing. "They give their wishes to me, willingly, and I make it so they forget their worries."

Tears blurred Asha's vision, but she didn't back down. "You make it so they forget the most beautiful part of themselves!"

The king paused, listening.

"And they don't know what they're missing. But you do. And now I do," said Asha, her voice wavering. "It's not fair. My saba is good. The people of Rosas are good. They deserve more than just false hope. And no matter how hard the journey might be, they deserve a chance—"

King Magnifico spun to face her, magic swirling in his hands. "*I* decide what everyone deserves," he growled.

A bell suddenly rang, startling them both. Then they heard Queen Amaya's voice. "Mi rey?" she called, which meant *my king* in Spanish. When she saw Asha in the observatory, the queen's mouth fell open in surprise. The king rarely brought guests into the wish chamber. "Sorry to interrupt. But it's time for the ceremony."

"Is it?" said the king. "My love, seat Asha with you on the main stage."

"Oh no," Asha protested. "No, no. That's okay—"

"I insist," declared the king. His piercing blue eyes bored into Asha.

A trickle of fear ran down her spine. She had challenged the king. What would he do in return?

Under a dusky blue sky, a band played a lively anthem. The people of Rosas cheered and waved flags in the air. But sitting onstage near Queen Amaya, Asha felt very much alone.

When King Magnifico stepped before the crowd, cheers erupted. "Are you ready, Rosas?" he asked. He spread his arms wide, sending magical beams of light radiating in all directions. Colorful clouds of confetti swooped overhead like a flock of birds. "Another beautiful night in my kingdom. So good to see you, good to be seen."

Asha searched the crowd and spotted her mother, her grandfather, and Valentino standing with Dahlia and the other teens. They waved at her excitedly.

But Asha was filled with dread. Tonight, more people would give their wishes to the king, wishes that he would likely lock away with no intention of granting. And he wouldn't grant Saba's wish, either—not ever!

The king's voice boomed out over the crowd. "First things first," he said. "We have two new citizens ready to give their wishes."

The crowd cheered when a young couple stepped up to the stage.

"Helena, Esteban," said the king, "you're going to be very happy here, I promise you." He swirled his palms, conjuring magical energy, and then clasped their outstretched hands. At his touch, their hearts began to glow. The light rushed down their arms and into their cupped palms, transforming into glowing wish bubbles.

When King Magnifico took the wishes, the glow left Helena's and Esteban's bodies. Their shoulders slumped, and their smiles faded.

"It's a real weight off, isn't it?" said King Magnifico. He shot Asha a smug look, reveling in his power.

Asha could only watch, her heart breaking.

"Forget without regret!" cheered the crowd.

As Esteban and Helena forgot their wishes, their expressions changed again. They waved happily to the audience before leaving the stage.

"Okay then," the king bellowed, "who is ready to have their wish granted?"

The crowd went wild, and everyone sneaked glances at Sabino.

"Now," said the king, raising his finger to quiet the crowd, "I have been challenged today to take a chance and try something new. Thank you, Asha."

She met his cold gaze, wondering what cruel trick he was about to play.

The king turned back to his adoring crowd. "And it is with clarity and an open heart full of love that I grant today's wish to someone who has very patiently waited long enough!"

"Sabino," voices murmured. "It has to be Sabino."

Sabino laughed nervously, his cheeks pink with hope that his wish might be granted. But Asha knew better.

"Sania Osman," King Magnifico announced. "Where is Sania? There she is. Come on up, Sania. Please come forward."

A ripple of shock ran through the crowd. The king hadn't chosen Sabino! Asha squeezed her eyes shut.

Sania Osman squealed with excitement. "He said *Sania*?" she asked. "It's me? It's me. It's me!" She pumped her fists in the air.

As Sakina tried to comfort Sabino, lucky Sania scrambled through the crowd toward the stage. She tripped in her excitement, but others helped her back up. "Coming through, thank you!" she cried. "It's just so exciting!"

"Sania Osman!" said King Magnifico as she rushed up the stairs toward him. "I mean it when I say it truly is my great pleasure to grant your heart's desire."

"Oh my," murmured Sania as he held up her wish.

"To sew the most beautiful dresses in all the lands!" declared the king.

As the crowd gasped in delight, the wish bubble swirled around Sania, encircling her in shimmering light. A golden pair of shears floated gently into her hands. "My wish has come true . . . ," she said incredulously.

"This is thrilling!" cried someone from the crowd.

"So wonderful!" cried another.

But around Saba Sabino, other voices murmured with disappointment.

"Poor Saba," said Dahlia.

"He's waited so long," agreed Simon.

"See?" said grumpy Gabo. "Never ever get your hopes up."

Sakina pulled Sabino into a hug. "I'm so sorry, Saba," she said. Even Valentino cast a sad glance at the old man.

"Let's hear it for Sania Osman!" exclaimed the king.

While Queen Amaya gave Sania a congratulatory hug, King Magnifico shot Asha a look of satisfaction. "Asha, obviously I will not be offering you the position as my apprentice," he said. "But don't worry. I will still protect your saba's wish and your mother's—forever." His promise sounded more like a threat.

When Queen Amaya overheard the king's strange promise, she followed the king off the stage. "Mi rey?" she said.

The king ignored her confused expression. "Now that went well, don't you think?" he boasted. "Are you hungry?"

Asha was left sitting alone. She had questioned the king, and for that, he was punishing her—and her family. She sank into her chair in despair.

Chapter Five

That night, Asha, Sakina, and Saba sat around the dinner table in heavy silence. Asha's heart ached with sadness. Even Valentino seemed too upset to climb. The little goat rested beside Asha, his head on her lap.

"Come now, we don't want to waste food," said Sabino, gesturing toward his birthday cake. Sakina had decorated it with a smiley face made of berries. "Dig in . . . and enjoy!" He poured Sakina a cup of tea.

"You're right, Saba," said Sakina. "We should be looking at the bright side. Asha, you got to the final few being considered for the most prestigious position in the kingdom. And, Saba, there's always next time."

"Cheers to that," said Sabino, raising his cup. Sakina toasted him with a *clink,* but Asha remained still.

"Asha . . . ?" said Sakina.

Asha finally met her grandfather's gaze. "Saba," she said, "I need to tell you something."

"Tell me what, child?" he asked.

Asha forced the words out. "I don't think, um, your wish will ever be granted."

Sakina's eyes widened. "Why would you say such a thing?" she asked.

"Because the king told me so," said Asha, her heart heavy. "He said it's too dangerous to grant."

Sabino's brow furrowed. "My wish is dangerous?"

"No," said Asha quickly. "That's the thing. I don't think it is at all—"

"You saw it?" Sakina asked incredulously.

"I did," Asha admitted. She turned to Saba. "And you should know what it is."

"No, no," Sabino protested. "Don't say anything—"

Asha took his hand. "But it's so, so beautiful," she said, remembering the joyful wish.

Her grandfather pulled his hand away. "Well, clearly Magnifico feels otherwise," he said, "so—"

"Saba, what gives him the right to decide?" Asha countered.

"He . . . ," Sabino faltered, searching for words. "He is the king, and he has made everything possible for us."

"But he—" began Asha.

"When your father passed, he made sure we were taken care of," Sabino reminded her.

"But he could have granted your wishes," said Asha. "Wouldn't that have helped more?"

"We can't know these things," Sabino said firmly.

"If you had seen them," said Asha, "if you had felt them like I did, you would understand!" She stood, imploring her family to listen. "It's not just yours, Saba. There are so many wondrous, powerful wishes that will never be granted—"

"Asha," Sakina said in warning, willing her to stop.

"Just floating there—" said Asha, her voice rising.

"Asha!" her mother said sharply.

"Helpless," Asha finished.

"Sit down," her mother pleaded. "Calm down."

"I can't!" Asha blurted. "I can't just sit here with you, Saba, knowing your incredible wish and not tell you—"

"Then don't," said Sabino. His usually kind face had hardened.

"What?" said Asha.

"You are excused from the table," he ordered.

"Saba?" Asha's stomach dropped.

When he spoke again, Asha could hear the pain in his voice. "Why?" he asked. "Why would you want me to know a wish that can never be?"

"But I didn't . . ." Asha tried to explain. "But it's your wish!"

"Are you trying to break my heart, child?" asked Sabino. He stood to meet her eyes.

Asha sank back down. "No. No. I would never ever

try . . . ," she said. "I'm sorry." Before she could cause Saba another ounce of pain, she lunged from her seat and rushed out the front door.

"Asha," her mother called from the doorway. "Asha!"

But Asha kept running. Heartbroken, she raced down the shadowy path from the cottage, with Valentino scampering behind.

Night was falling when Asha paused to catch her breath. She knew the truth about King Magnifico now, but it felt like a weight on her shoulders. She wished she could show the people of Rosas the beauty of the wishes—and the ugliness of the king's lies. Would that change their minds about him?

Asha considered what to do as she crossed a moss-covered bridge. She wanted to tell the townspeople the truth, but her mother and Saba had already tried to silence her. Asha knew she was young, but she also knew right from wrong. And what the king was doing was wrong.

She looked up at the stars for guidance as she walked toward the city of Rosas. The king had granted many wishes. But as Asha and Valentino entered the marketplace, she noticed all the citizens who were still waiting for Magnifico to grant theirs.

That man on the porch. What was his forgotten wish? Asha knew—he wanted to become an underwater explorer. The woman sweeping the cobblestones.

What was her wish? To be a captain at the helm of a great ship. That woman feeding the birds? Asha knew that her wish was to fly with them.

Asha's heart ached knowing that these people had given away the most beautiful parts of themselves. They could have so much more, if only . . .

She glanced skyward, yearning for something to point her in the right direction. One bright star twinkled, as if listening. That gave Asha an idea. She ran up the staircase toward the balcony overlooking all of Rosas. Her eyes landed on the wishing tree.

Asha knew now what she needed to do—what her father had taught her. She raced toward the wishing tree, climbed the gnarled trunk, and perched on a branch. As Valentino settled in beside her, she gazed at the twinkling star above. Then she made her wish: for the people of Rosas to have more than what the king had chosen for them.

As soon as Asha's wish left her lips, the bright star flashed with a blinding burst of light. Then, like a brilliant comet, it raced through the sky toward Rosas.

Magical light swept across the kingdom of Rosas. It bathed Asha and the wishing tree in a warm glow and then sped through the forest, where animals chirped and chattered in wonder.

The light flooded Asha's cottage. Sabino gazed out the window and closed his eyes, drinking in the sweet sensation. "Oh, can you feel that?" he asked Sakina.

The light swept across the hamlet and through Dahlia's room, where she sat in bed reading. She laughed with joy. The light enveloped Queen Amaya on the castle balcony, too. She hugged herself, embracing the incredible feeling.

But when the light reached the observatory, the king startled. "Wha . . . ?" The wishes overhead vibrated and swirled, racing around the domed ceiling. They made a harmonious sound, like a symphony striking a chord.

"What's happening?" the king cried in a panic. "No. No, no, no. . . ." What had caused the light? And what was it doing to the wishes?

The light spread all across the island of Rosas. Then, in an instant, it retracted into a single point of light in the forest. Darkness followed. Now, the only glow came from the moon and stars.

Back in the observatory, the wish bubbles settled overhead as Queen Amaya entered the room. "Mi rey!" she gushed. "You spoil us with your magic. Whatever that was, it was marvelous."

King Magnifico, still filled with dread, stared up at the wishes. "I didn't do it," he confessed.

"What?" asked the queen. If the king hadn't summoned the magical light, who had?

"And it affected my wishes," said the king. "Is it some sort of warning?" He pondered that for a moment, and then stiffened with certainty. "I believe I have just been threatened."

"Who would dare threaten you?" asked Queen Amaya. The king was the most powerful sorcerer in the land . . . wasn't he?

Filled with an incredible feeling of hope, Asha climbed down from the wishing tree. "What was that?" she asked Valentino.

Just then, the goat spotted something: a golden light zigzagging through the brush behind Asha. "Baaa!" he called, leaping and bounding after the light.

"You felt it too, didn't you?" Asha asked Valentino as she turned toward the hamlet. "It was . . . electric!" She paused and leaned against a well, still feeling dreamy. "It was joy and hope, and possibility and wonder, inside the most loving light."

Behind her, the mysterious light zoomed around like a firefly. When it disappeared in the bushes, Valentino spun in a circle trying to find it—until the light darted out and dragged him into the bushes, too.

"Can light be loving?" Asha continued. "I sound ridiculous, don't I?" She looked around for Valentino, but the goat was gone. "I'll take that as a yes."

Swoosh! A streak of light zipped past Asha, with Valentino bounding playfully after it.

"Whoa! Whoa!" cried Asha. "Valentino!" She raced after the goat.

The light flashed through the woods toward the hamlet. Asha and Valentino followed it to where the light dove into a pair of knit pajamas hanging on a clothesline.

Asha held out her hands. "Stay back," she warned Valentino. "Shh."

With the light stuck in the rear, the pajama bottoms seemed to be dancing all on their own. "Creepy," said Asha.

Then the light flew into the collar, pulling the pajamas upright. "Oh!" said Asha, leaning back as the pajamas stood to face her. A tiny, bright limb popped out of the collar and tapped Asha's nose. *Boop!*

Then the light took off, whisking the pajamas away with it. "Wait!" cried Asha. She grabbed a pajama leg, but the light tugged in the other direction, unraveling the pajamas. "No, no, no, no . . . ," Asha protested. She kept hold of the yarn as the light pulled her through the forest. With one final tug, the light pulled the yarn away and disappeared through an opening in the thicket.

Valentino was already ducking through the thicket, so Asha crawled in, too. What choice did she have?

CHAPTER SIX

When Asha stepped into the clearing, she spotted Valentino playing a game with the light. The glowing orb zipped around a grove of trees, weaving red yarn around the branches and trunks in an intricate pattern. Rabbits, deer, and other forest animals crept from the brush to watch.

When the light spotted Asha, it dropped the yarn, as if surprised to see her.

"Um, okay," she murmured.

The light zoomed toward Asha and hovered before her, studying her face like a curious puppy.

"Ah! H-ho there," Asha stammered. She leaned away to get a better look. The glowing orb was the size of a lemon. It had an expressive, friendly face. When it floated too close, Asha raised her hands protectively. The light ran across her fingers with its bottom limbs.

"One, two, three, four, five . . . ," Asha whispered, counting the pointed limbs.

The light twirled around in Asha's ropelike belt, making her laugh. Then it shot behind her and snatched her journal, which it promptly opened.

"Wait," Asha commanded. "What are you doing? That is private." She tugged on her journal. When the light let go, the journal smacked Asha in the face. "Ow!" she cried.

Next, the light swept over to Valentino. It lifted the goat's ears and nibbled on his tail. When Valentino wiggled his rear, trying to shake it off, the light hung on, as if enjoying the ride. "Baaa!" Valentino responded in complaint.

Asha watched the light in wonder. "What . . . what *are* you?" she asked.

The light zipped into the canopy of trees, where the red yarn was still strung.

"You kind of look like . . . ," Asha began. Then she saw that the yarn in the trees formed a five-pointed shape. "A star," she finished breathlessly.

The light floated back down, smiling wide.

"Okay, you can't be!" said Asha, laughing at the very idea. "I mean, I know I wished on a . . . but—no. Yes?"

As if to verify Asha's guess, Star did loop the loops, sprinkling stardust all around. When the stardust settled on a patch of mushrooms, they came to life, stretching and yawning as if waking from a long nap.

"This is crazy," said Asha. Valentino was dazzled by the sparkly mushrooms.

"We love crazy!" answered the mushrooms.

Asha gasped. "Ah, I'm seeing things," she said.

"Baaa!" Valentino bleated at Star, asking for more magic. Star happily obliged, sprinkling the goat with stardust. Valentino stuck out his tongue to catch the dust like snowflakes.

"Whoa!" said Asha. "What are you doing? Valentino, don't eat that."

Valentino bleated again, then plopped down on his rump looking discouraged. So Star sprinkled more stardust on the goat. This time, when Valentino tried to bleat, something else came out—a human *voice.*

"It didn't work," said Valentino in a deep, booming voice. "When does the magic happen?"

Asha sucked in her breath.

When Valentino realized he had spoken, he raised a hoof to his mouth in surprise. "Ah!"

"Oh, something's happened . . . ," Asha murmured.

"I'm talking!" Valentino declared. "I am *talking*! Who knew my voice would be this low?" He seemed quite pleased with himself.

Asha, feeling bewildered, looked again at Star. But the magical light was only just getting started.

Star zipped toward some flowers and sprinkled them with stardust. Instantly, the blossoms came to life and began dancing. Then Star "woke up" a large tree.

As Star spread stardust on a squirrel, a porcupine, and a rabbit, the forest animals chattered in wonder.

"Delicious."

"Mmm. Magic is chewy."

"Sparkly and spicy."

Astonished, Asha blurted, "Okay, I have a few thousand questions, starting with how did I manage to connect with a star all the way across the sky and ending with how is *any* of this possible?"

"Relax," said the rabbit. "To all your questions there is one very simple answer."

"Which is . . . ?" asked Asha.

"Think about it," said the bushy-tailed squirrel. "We're no different, you and me. We are all . . ." The squirrel paused, waiting for Asha to guess.

"Overwhelmed?" Asha offered.

Star giggled at her answer.

"And completely, entirely made of the very same, very special thing," the rabbit continued, gesturing toward Star. "Which is . . . ?"

Asha stared at Star, trying to describe how the glowing orb made her feel. "Hope?" she guessed again.

The forest animals groaned.

"Let's try this another way," said the squirrel.

With help from the plants, trees, and other animals, the squirrel began to show Asha that every living thing on Earth was connected, because we are all made of stardust! Trees—from a sapling to a stump—explained how stardust turned seeds into full-grown plants. An owl landed before Asha, its eyes like tiny galaxies filled with bright stars. From rabbits to bears, turtles to deer, racoons to feathery quail, forest friends surrounded Asha and helped her see that we are more alike than we realize.

As the enchanted animals surrounded Asha, she saw that their hearts glowed with stardust. And when Star gently touched her chest, her heart began to glow. Now Asha understood: Since everything is made of stardust, the power of the stars is accessible to everyone!

Asha felt just as energized as the forest animals now. When Star perched atop her head, Asha grinned. "This is extraordinary," she said. "My father said that we were connected to the stars. That's why I wished, and . . . now you're here . . . for me . . . ?"

Star tumbled off her head and hovered before her, looking joyful.

"Well, what do I . . . Wait, do you *grant* wishes?" Asha asked.

Star frowned and turned upside down.

"Oh no, I'm sorry. Obviously not," said Asha. "Forget I asked."

Star, now fascinated with Asha, drew on her chin with glowing stardust.

"I'm just not sure how this works," said Asha. "I wished for more for us, for my family and for—"

Star suddenly righted itself. Asha worried she'd said something wrong. "Oh no, no, no," she said quickly. "Not in, like, a selfish way. I just want their wishes to have a chance."

At that, Star kicked its legs, as if in full agreement.

Asha gestured toward the castle and then pulled out her journal. "But, um, look"—she showed Star the drawing she'd made of the wish chamber—"King Magnifico has their wishes in the castle, captured in these ball-like bubbly things that are very beautiful but very locked up, and he'll never give them back."

Star flinched at the thought, and then took off like a shot. It zoomed around and gathered the yarn from the trees.

"Wha . . . what are you doing?" Asha called.

"Careful!" Valentino warned. "My mother was shaved for that yarn!"

Star wound the yarn into a ball and tucked it into Asha's hands. Then Star glanced eagerly at the castle and back at Asha as if trying to tell her something.

"Yes, that's the castle," said Asha, not understanding. Then she saw the emotion in Star's expression. Star wanted the wishes to be free, too! "You mean we take them back ourselves?" Asha asked.

Star gave her a mischievous smile.

"But if we take them, isn't that stealing?" asked Asha. "I mean, we can't—"

Star blew out a puff of stardust in protest.

"Right," said Asha. "They don't belong to him, do they?"

Star tugged on the yarn and gestured toward the castle, as if to say, "Let's go!"

"Well, okay," said Asha. "But . . ."

Star spun around Asha with the yarn and then zipped on ahead. "Wait. Wait!" Asha cried, running after Star. "Slow down. We need a plan!"

Valentino suddenly fell from a tree branch above and scampered after them. "I'm coming!" he called in his gruff goat voice. "Wait for me!"

Chapter Seven

King Magnifico stood in his study amidst piles of books. Convinced that someone must have used magic to create the mysterious light, he was searching his spell books for answers.

"What was it?" the king cried. "What was it? Who could have commanded it?" He tugged at the pages of a book in rage. "Why is there *nothing*?!" He threw the book across the room into the roaring flames of the hearth.

"Mi rey, what is happening in here?" asked Queen Amaya as she entered.

"I don't know who we're dealing with," said King Magnifico, "and these books are useless!" He'd looked through every book he owned—all but one. He hurried toward the glass case that protected the forbidden book.

"What are you doing—" began the queen cautiously.

The king cut her off. "To summon such light would demand a spell so powerful," he murmured to himself. He waved his hands, and the etched hornets on the glass came to life, unlocking the case for him.

"No," warned Amaya. "You yourself say 'Forbidden magic is not the way.' "

But the king had already grabbed the book. The stone embedded in the book's cover glowed green with an ominous energy. "A king must be prepared to do anything to protect his kingdom," said Magnifico.

"Prepared, yes," agreed Amaya. "Impulsive, no." She carefully approached the king. "You are not that powerless boy you were. You are a mighty sorcerer who commands great magic. But this book . . ." She studied his face in concern. "With it, you know you risk magic controlling *you.*"

The king hesitated, but he didn't put the book down.

"Your people and the wishes are unharmed," the queen reminded him.

"For now," said the king.

"Well then, for now, please put that book down," the queen begged. She placed her hand gently on his shoulder.

The king finally set the book back in the case. With a wave of his hand, the hornets buzzed back to the glass, locking the book safely inside.

Queen Amaya led the king toward the window and

drew open the curtains. "You are the greatest protector of Rosas," she reassured him. "If you want answers about that light, I suggest you start with your people."

He gazed out over his beautiful, busy kingdom.

"They love you," said the queen in a soothing voice.

"I know," the king answered.

"They would do anything for you," the queen crooned.

"Of course they would," the king agreed.

"You are their handsomest, most beloved sorcerer-king," the queen continued.

"You're right," said King Magnifico. "I am a handsome king." Finally, he smiled and pulled the queen into an embrace. "Oh, my love, excellent advice. Rosas is so lucky to have you, as am I."

Queen Amaya gently kissed the king's hand. King Magnifico gazed out over his kingdom—his people—with pride.

As Asha and Valentino hurried through the marketplace, Asha's pouch wriggled in her hands. She peeked inside, where a playful Star was tangled up in yarn.

"Can you stop squiggling, please?" Asha pleaded. "You're drawing attention."

Asha weaved her way through the crowd. "Hi. Hello. I'm just gonna . . ." She felt Star wiggling inside the bag as she squeezed between shoppers. "I have to go to the bathroom!" she fibbed, and the crowd parted to make way for her. She broke into a run and raced toward the castle, eager to get inside.

Finally, she and Valentino reached the chicken room adjacent to the castle kitchen. Chickens clucked from their nesting boxes and perches as Asha quickly closed the door. She caught her breath and then opened the squirming pouch. "Okay, you can come out now."

Star popped out sporting a red outfit woven from yarn. The top was so tight, it barely covered Star's round belly. Asha couldn't help but laugh. "Are those pajamas?" she asked.

Valentino admired Star's new pajamas, which were clearly inspired by his own pair. "Thank you," he said, his gruff voice wavering with emotion. "I feel seen."

"Okay, focus," said Asha, getting down to business. "I need to talk to Dahlia." Asha cracked the door open and peered toward the kitchen. "There has to be a way to sneak into the king's study—"

Crash! Behind Asha, Star was joyfully pushing items off a shelf.

"Without anyone seeing you," Asha continued as Valentino caught a jar and a bottle in the basket that had landed on his head.

"Yes, yes, I'm way ahead of you," agreed Valentino. "Star may alarm the masses."

"Much like a talking goat," Asha added with a smile.

"What?" bleated Valentino, offended.

"Which is why you're both staying here," Asha declared.

"With the chickens?" screeched Valentino. "Did you see what just came out of that one's b—"

Asha cut him off. "I'll be right back," she promised. "Stay quiet."

She closed the door and tiptoed toward the kitchen, where she saw Gabo, Hal, and Safi eating cookies while Simon snoozed with his head on the counter.

"Even you have to admit, Gabo," gushed Hal, "that light last night felt amazing."

"It was probably a curse," Gabo grumbled.

As Dahlia pulled a fresh batch of cookies from the oven, the teens crowded around, ready for more. Even sleepy Simon reached out his hand for a cookie.

"No," said Dahlia, pulling the tray away. "This batch is for the king!"

The teens groaned, and Simon slumped back into sleep. Then Dario entered the room from the other direction. "A squirrel just said good morning to me," he said, baffled.

"As squirrels do," Gabo said sarcastically.

Dario's eyes widened. "Really?" he said, thinking Gabo was being serious. "Huh. First for me."

"Seriously," Gabo muttered to Dahlia, "he wouldn't survive without us."

Crash! Another horrific sound came from the chicken room, sending the teens' attention toward where Asha stood. To cover it up, Asha intentionally bumped into a nearby stack of copper pots. "Oh, I really have to watch where I'm going," she said to the teens, who were all staring now.

"Hey, you touch 'em, you wash 'em," grumbled Gabo.

"It was an accident, Gabo," said Bazeema, who had suddenly appeared next to him.

Gabo gasped. "Ah! Where did you . . . How are you doing that?"

Bazeema only shrugged.

Dahlia hurried toward Asha, who was picking up the pots. "Hey," Dahlia said kindly, "how are you and your poor saba this morning?"

"Coping," said Asha. She was still worried about Saba, but she had so much more to worry about now! She casually changed the subject. "And curious. How do the kitchens get food up to the king?"

"Oh, um . . ." Dahlia paused, surprised by the question. "The formal servers bring his meals to the dining room."

Valentino's deep laughter suddenly burst from the

chicken room, along with a *bawk, bawk, bawk.* Asha tried to cover it up by laughing loudly, as if Dahlia had said something hilarious. Then she pressed Dahlia for more information. "So what about when the king eats in his study? Who brings it then?"

Dahlia peered at Asha through her wire-rimmed glasses. "Well, his study is off-limits." She cleared her throat and added, "Details are known to only a select few."

"Including you?" Asha asked.

Dahlia cast her a sideways glance. "No comment."

Asha sucked in her breath. Dahlia *did* know a way into the study.

Zing! A magical sound emerged from the chicken room, followed by *cluck, cluck, cluck, cluck, cluck!*

"Ladies, please," said Valentino, his voice muffled by the closed door. "Everyone will get a turn. Form a line, preferably by height."

Dahlia heard the gruff voice and saw a flash of light through the crack in the door. "Who is in there?" she asked, stepping toward the door.

"I don't hear anything," Asha fibbed, steering Dahlia away. Then she leaned closer to her friend. "Dahlia, if you know a secret way into the king's study, you *have* to tell me."

"Why? What is going on with you?" Dahlia asked pointedly, looking at her friend with suspicion.

Achoo! When Safi headed toward the chicken room with an egg basket, Asha rushed ahead of him and plastered herself against the door. "Whoa, wait, wait, wait! What are you doing?" she asked.

"I gotta collect eggs," said Safi.

"No! I mean, let me. I'll do it for you." Asha reached for the basket.

"Nah, that's okay, Asha," said Safi.

She thought fast. "But your allergies!"

The other teens in the room, who could tell something was up, gathered around.

"Are you trying to take the chickens away from me?" asked Safi, growing teary.

"You know Safi loves those chickens," said Bazeema.

"I do," Safi sniffled.

Dahlia studied Asha's face. "Are you okay, Asha?" she asked, cocking her head in curiosity.

"Something's up with you," added Gabo, crossing his arms.

Even upbeat Hal was suspicious. "What are you hiding?"

More noises and clucks sounded from the chicken room.

"Nothing," Asha insisted.

"That's it—life is to be *lived*!" declared Valentino from behind the closed door.

"And nobody," Asha added. She pressed herself

against the door, but she wouldn't be able to keep her friends out for much longer.

"What is going on in there?" Dahlia demanded to know.

"You look really guilty," said Dario.

"Friends shouldn't hide things from each other," Hal pointed out.

"Move or we break the door down!" threatened Gabo.

"No, no, no. Fine!" said Asha in a rush. "Last night, after everything happened, I made a wish . . . on a star."

The teens stared at her, and Gabo smirked. "What are you? Five?" he asked. "Stop stalling!"

"No, listen!" said Asha. "And the star answered." She couldn't explain to her friends what she meant. She would have to show them.

Asha took a deep breath and opened the door.

Chapter Eight

Star and Valentino had turned the chicken room into a musical *eggs*travaganza! Thanks to Star's magic, the chickens weren't squawking—they were *singing.* And dancing! They lined up in choreographed rows, flapping their wings and kicking in unison.

Valentino conducted them as if they were a choir, using a feather as a baton. "That's it, ladies," said the goat. "Your wings can't fly, but your voices can!"

When Asha's friends saw the talking goat and singing chickens, their jaws dropped. "Wow," uttered Dario. "I have *really* been underestimating animals."

The dancing chickens circled around Asha and her bewildered friends. But where was Star? Asha searched the room.

"Amazing, one stick to command them all!" said Valentino, using a piece of hay as a makeshift baton. "Okay, big finish!"

The chickens ended their performance in a feathery flurry of energy. Then Star burst through the circle of chickens.

At the sight of the glowing star, the teens gasped. When Safi's gasp turned into the start of a sneeze, everyone held a finger under his nose to stop it.

"These are my friends," Asha said to Star.

Star studied each teen's face—except for Gabo, who ducked and hid. When Star hovered in front of Dahlia, her face lit up. "Wow. My whole understanding of the natural world is completely turned upside down," she said. "And yet I'm fine with it."

Star reached out to tap Dahlia's nose. *Boop!*

Then Star plucked the glasses off her face and tried them on. But Star couldn't see a thing! When Star accidentally bumped into Hal, the teen grinned. Star smiled, too, and reached out to boop her nose.

"I've never felt so happy in all my life," said Hal, breathless. "And that's saying something."

Star floated near Bazeema next and booped her nose. She waved shyly and giggled, then ducked behind Hal. That made Star giggle, too.

Then it was Safi's turn. *Boop!* Star tapped his nose, which made Safi sneeze. *Achoo!* Instantly, Star knit a handkerchief for Safi out of red yarn.

Safi wiped his nose. "Much better than my sleeve," he said. "Thanks."

Star hovered near Dario next. But Dario was holding a chicken, trying to figure out where the eggs came from. He didn't notice the glowing orb until Star tapped his nose. *Boop!*

"Oh, hey," said Dario. "Thanks."

Next, Star zoomed toward Simon. Hovering in front of the sleepy teen, Star's expression changed from confusion to concern. Star reached out to stroke Simon's forehead, as if feeling sorry for the teen.

"What?" Simon asked Asha. "Why do I make it sad?"

Star glanced at Asha with a questioning expression, and suddenly, she understood.

"Oh, well . . . ," Asha said to Star, "Simon's eighteen. He's already given his wish to the king."

Simon's face fell. "You can feel it?" he asked Star. "I can't remember what I lost."

Star crocheted a little heart for Simon. Then Star spotted Gabo, who was still hiding. Thinking that the teen was playing a game, Star tried to get closer, but Gabo dodged away.

"Ah. Stay away. Nope. Nope!" exclaimed Gabo. "Am I the only one who realizes this is going to end very badly?"

"Not if everyone keeps quiet about Star," Asha insisted.

Star spun around Asha to surprise Gabo, like a game

of peekaboo, but Gabo ducked away again. "Magic is forbidden by anyone other than Magnifico, our *king*," said Gabo, "who is also the only one authorized to grant wishes."

"*Self*-authorized," Asha pointed out.

"Does Star grant wishes?" asked Simon, who was still thinking about the wish he'd given up.

"No," said Asha, "but it does seem to want to help me pursue mine."

"Like a fairy godmother," said Dario, who was now holding the chicken upside down, inspecting its underside.

Just then, Star caught up with Gabo and gave him a bright smile. Gabo's eyes widened in awe, then he shook his head. "Life is not a fairy tale," he reminded himself.

"Depends on how you look at it," said Hal. "But maybe it could be."

"What did you wish for?" Gabo asked Asha. "No, don't tell us. I want no part in this."

When trumpets blared from the courtyard, the teens exchanged worried looks. "That's the king's call to assemble," said Bazeema.

Asha knew that Magnifico was about to make a royal announcement. Would the announcement be about the magical light—about Star? Her stomach twisted.

"Please," Asha begged her friends. "Magnifico can't know about Star."

When no one responded, Asha tried to reassure them. "I promise you, my wish won't harm or affect any of you or Rosas."

"That's a big promise, Asha," Simon pointed out.

"But we trust you," Hal assured her. "Don't we, Bazee—" She glanced around the kitchen. "Where'd she go?"

"How does she do that?" said Gabo with a scowl.

When the trumpets sounded again, Hal held up her hands. "It's okay," she said. "We won't tell anyone, Asha."

"No one would believe me, anyway," said Dario with a shrug.

"We got you," Safi told Asha. "Right, Gabo?" Safi gave Gabo a pointed look as they left the kitchen.

"I am not happy to be put in this position," said Gabo, "but I don't squeal."

Soon, only Dahlia and Asha remained in the chicken room. Dahlia looked Asha firmly in the eye and asked, "What are you not telling me?"

"Okay, okay," Asha responded. "Yesterday, I kind of challenged the king."

"What?" Dahlia gasped.

"It's, uh, complicated," said Asha.

"And . . . ?" asked Dahlia, pressing for more details.

Asha hesitated, trying to decide how much to tell her best friend. "Dahlia," she began, "what would *you* do if you found out the wishes of those you love with all your heart will never be granted?"

"You mean your saba's wish," Dahlia said gently.

"And, thanks to me, my mother's," Asha explained. "I'm here to get their wishes so I can give them back to them."

"You're here to *steal* from the king?" asked Dahlia.

Star zoomed to Asha's defense and shook its entire body, as if to say, "No, no, no!"

"It's not stealing," Asha echoed. How could she make Dahlia understand? "The wishes don't belong to him."

"And you can't just ask Magnifico for them back?" Dahlia suggested.

"I think I've ruined my chances of asking Magnifico for anything," said Asha with a sigh.

Dahlia saw the pain in her friend's eyes. She then led Asha toward a cabinet and slid it open. "This is how we get food to the king's study," she explained, pointing toward a dumbwaiter. The box had pulleys—ropes used to raise and lower it.

"It's perfect," said Asha, giving Dahlia a grateful hug.

Asha crawled into the dumbwaiter with Star and squeezed to the side so that Valentino could fit, too.

"A new way to climb!" raved Valentino. "Backing up." He entered the dumbwaiter rump first.

Asha leaned away from the goat's squirming rear. "Okay, look out!" she cried as his behind moved toward her. "We can't fit. Oh, ugh."

"Are you sure about this?" asked Dahlia. "Magnifico could come back any time."

"And that's why you're going to stall him," said Asha. She flashed Dahlia a smile. "Please and thank you, best friend ever?"

Dahlia raised her eyebrows. "How am I supposed to stall a king?!"

"You'll think of something," Asha assured her. "You're a genius!" She slid the dumbwaiter door closed before Dahlia could protest.

"Let's go up!" Valentino urged.

"I have to reach the pulley thing." Asha nudged Valentino aside and fumbled for the rope, giving it a tug.

"And we ride!" Valentino shouted. "I'm sorry, that was right in your ear."

As Asha pulled the rope, the dumbwaiter slowly squeaked upward.

CHAPTER NINE

When King Magnifico and Queen Amaya appeared on the steps of the castle, excited murmurs rose from the courtyard:

"Can't believe that light last night."

"That light was amazing."

"Like nothing I've ever seen!"

As Dahlia pushed through the crowd toward her friends, the king called everyone to attention. "Quiet, quiet, quiet!" he commanded. "I know you are all wondering about that little light last night."

At the mention of the light, the crowd went wild, which only annoyed the king. "A light I did not command or condone!" he quickly clarified.

The cheering stopped, and confusion rippled through the courtyard.

"It was magic," said Magnifico, "though quite clumsy

and amateurish. It was also completely forbidden. There is a traitor amongst us who defied the law. They used magic to put you all at risk!"

Shocked townspeople whispered to one another.

"But don't worry," the king said soothingly. "They are no match for me, and I assure you, when caught, they will be punished severely."

Dahlia and the teens exchanged guilty looks. Then Dahlia glanced up at the windows of the observatory. Had Asha reached the wishes? And could she make it back out without getting caught?

Asha grunted as she pulled on the dumbwaiter cord. Her arms were tired.

"You are awfully slow at this," Valentino said in complaint.

Finally, Asha heard a click and the *ding* of a bell. "Shh," she said. "I think we're here."

"Adventure awaits right outside this door!" said Valentino loudly.

"Let's go," said Asha. But when she tried to slide the door open, it wouldn't budge. "Oh no. No, no, no, no. It's locked."

"I'll ram it," Valentino offered. He butted his head against the door. "Ow! It hurts without horns."

Star shot a bright limb through a crack in the wood and tossed stardust around. But the magic missed the lock and landed on the king's desk instead.

"What are you doing?" Asha asked Star.

A quill enchanted with stardust hopped out of the inkwell and skated around the desk, covering a piece of parchment with inky swirls.

"Star, please don't break anything," Asha warned.

"But don't hold back!" said Valentino encouragingly. "Trust your inner goat."

Star made another attempt to send its magic through the crack, but the stardust missed the lock again. This time, a skull came to life and began eating the parchment on the desk. Then a magnifying glass jumped up and caught the sunlight, setting the parchment on fire!

"What's happening?" cried Asha, hearing the commotion outside the door.

"Just go all out," Valentino told Star. "Throw magic dust everywhere! It'll be fine."

Star stuck a limb through the crack one last time. At last, the stardust hit the lock. The bolt stretched as if waking from a nap and popped out of the slot, opening the dumbwaiter door.

"Yes!" cried Asha—until she saw that the king's desk was on fire. "No!"

"Ah!" bleated Valentino.

So far, their secret mission had *not* gone as planned. Hopefully Dahlia could stall the king a bit longer.

In the courtyard, townspeople were reeling from the news that there was a traitor in their midst. The king gestured to the crowd to calm down. "I ask you to keep your eyes and ears open," he instructed. "Any information would be most helpful. Rosas needs you. And I know you will never, ever let me down. Thank you."

As the king and queen turned to go, Dahlia panicked. Magnifico couldn't go back into the castle. What if he found Asha in his study? "Your Majesty, wait!" she cried, so loudly that townspeople stared.

The king peered curiously at the dark-haired teen in the bright red apron. "Yes, go on," he said.

Dahlia cleared her throat. "Hi, I'm Dahlia," she began. The handsome king was looking right at her. "Goodness, your eyes *are* that sparkly, objectively," she murmured, heat rising in her cheeks.

"What can I do for you, Dahlia?" asked the king impatiently.

"Thank you for asking," said Dahlia, pulling herself together. "You said 'any information' would be helpful. But pragmatically speaking, what qualifies? Evidentiary? How about circumstantial? Firsthand, secondhand . . . Well, then there's third—"

"How about hunches?" called out a tall man in the crowd.

"Thank you," said Dahlia, relieved that someone else had chimed in. "Though I doubt it. How about hunches?"

"Yes *any,*" said Magnifico. He pinched the bridge of his nose, as if irritated. "*Any* information about who or what caused the light would be helpful. So, yes, hunch. Hunch away."

The woman who often fed birds in the courtyard spoke up, too. "You said it was amateur magic, but then why don't you know how they did it?" she asked.

"What?" said the king, clearly annoyed.

"Oh, we're not going there—" said Dahlia, trying to stop what she had started.

"This is about what *you* know," said the king, trying to keep his voice calm. "It is about your safety and, most importantly, the safety of your wishes."

"Wait," blurted Simon from the crowd. "You mean our wishes aren't safe?"

Dahlia shot Simon a sharp look. As nervous whispers raced through the crowd, she tried to squelch them. "Of course they're safe!" she cried with a nervous laugh. But it was too late. The damage had been done.

Inside the king's study, Asha dumped a vase of flowers on the desk to put out the flaming scrolls. The water washed away the rest of the magic, too.

"Ha ha ha!" Valentino laughed appreciatively. "Good as new."

Asha threw several wet scrolls into the fireplace. "Hope he didn't need those," she muttered.

Star, who had just spotted its reflection in the mirror, squealed with delight. It made funny faces, stretching its mouth wide and squishing its cheeks.

"Okay, that's actually a door," said Asha, stepping toward the mirror. "And Magnifico waved his hand, and it just . . ." She waved, but nothing happened. "How about this . . . ?" She tried a bigger wave. "Nothing? Or this . . . ?" She raised her arm higher. "This?" She waved down low. "Or this?!" She flung her arm wide with an exaggerated wave, nearly toppling over.

Star imitated her by waving, and the mirror instantly opened to a doorway.

"Ha! Yes!" cried Asha, pumping her fists in the air.

"You got it!" cheered Valentino.

"Teamwork!" said Asha.

They raced into the observatory, with Star leading the way.

The wish bubbles hovered above, cloudy and indistinguishable. How would they possibly figure out which wishes belonged to Asha's family? As Star zoomed toward the bubbles, they circled around Star, as if greeting an old friend. One by one, Star touched each bubble and the cloudiness cleared, revealing the wishes inside: a man winning a trophy, someone holding a baby, a bodybuilder lifting weights . . .

Asha and Valentino craned their necks to see. "Wow," murmured Valentino. "The human imagination really is second to none but goat's."

By now, Star was bodysurfing across the sea of wishes as they lovingly passed it from one to the next.

"Star, I'm glad you're having fun," said Asha, "but you have to focus!" She opened her journal to a sketch of Sabino and Sakina and held it up. "Please find my saba's and mother's wishes," she pleaded. "As fast as you can!"

Star studied Asha's drawing and gave her a thumbs-up. But there were still hundreds of cloudy wishes. Could Star find the right ones before Magnifico returned?

In the courtyard, the crowd had whipped itself into a frenzy. "How do we know our wishes are safe?" asked an older woman with a ponytail. "We never see them!"

"Yes," said the bird lover. "Why can't we see them? Why is that a rule?"

"And why can't we remember them?" asked the tall man.

"Okay," said Dahlia, trying to calm everyone down. "We're getting *way* off topic."

"Since we're asking," said someone else in the crowd, "what if we want to change our wish?"

"Good point," added a woman with a hat. "Wishes can change."

"Wow," said Dahlia. "We don't have to start questioning everything, do we?" This was getting out of control!

"You know what would comfort us all the most?" said a man. "Another wish ceremony."

Everyone chimed in:

"Great idea!"

"Please, Your Majesty!"

"We could do it now!"

"No! Not now!" cried Dahlia. "Bad timing!"

But the voices in the crowd drowned her out. "Oh, please! Please! Please! Please, Your Majesty!" the crowd begged.

"Silence!" the rattled king ordered, raising his hands. "Is that all you can think about? A wish-granting ceremony?"

The crowd fell silent, but the hopeful looks on their faces said *yes*.

The king grabbed his head in his hands. "Fine," he

conceded. "Whoever identifies the traitor, your wish will be granted!"

As the crowd went wild, Simon leaned toward Dahlia. "Offering to grant a wish? He must really be worried."

"But hear this!" the king went on. "Anyone who helps the traitor, anyone who lets me down, your wish will *never* be granted!"

As rumbles of worry swept through the crowd, the teens exchanged nervous glances.

"Might I suggest," said Gabo through gritted teeth, "you all try not to look so guilty."

Dario struggled to wipe the guilty expression from his face and ended up looking dopey—his eyes crossed and tongue hanging out.

When the king marched back toward the castle, Dahlia cried out after him. "Wait! Your Majesty! Please, what qualifies as letting you down? Top five!"

But the crowd was too loud now. The king didn't hear.

Through the window of the observatory, Asha saw Magnifico leaving the courtyard. She looked up in a panic. "Star, he's coming," she cried. "Hurry!"

But there were still so many wishes to search through! Too many wishes. How would they ever find Sakina's and Saba's wishes in time?

CHAPTER TEN

King Magnifico burst through the doors into the castle hallway. "How brazenly they question me!" he thundered, his cape snapping behind him.

Queen Amaya followed, trying to soothe the king. "They only question you because you make them feel safe enough to do so," she offered.

But the king pulled away. "I'll be with the wishes," he growled. "Disturb me with nothing but good news."

As he stalked toward the observatory, he passed a model of Rosas, a miniature version of his kingdom. With a wave of his hand, Magnifico conjured tiny people to fill the town. Then he glared at them with contempt. How could the citizens of Rosas betray him when he took such good care of them?

He then stormed down a hallway lined with suits of armor. With a wave of his hand, the suits came to life and began to grovel at his feet. But the king marched on, still grumbling about his subjects' ingratitude. He let them live in the kingdom for free—he didn't even charge rent! He was always there to clean up their messes and listen to their troubles! And yet they wanted *more*?

As he marched upstairs toward his study, he passed a wall of mirrors. He stared at his reflection and wondered aloud, was it too much to ask for a little respect? Was this the thanks he got for everything he did for Rosas?

From inside the observatory, Asha heard the king's voice. She glanced nervously upward, where Star was still sorting through wishes. Would Star find her family's wishes in time?

The king's voice grew closer. Any moment now, he would discover them.

At last, Star found Sabino's wish! Star placed the precious bubble in Asha's hands. But before Star could look for Sakina's wish, Asha heard the door to the study burst open.

As Asha, Star, and Valentino rushed to hide, Magnifico walked toward the mirror in his study. He admired his reflection, which magically took on a life of its own, showering him with compliments. Then he waved a hand, and the door to the observatory slid open.

The king entered and he passed by his potions. He

didn't see Asha, Star, and Valentino hiding behind the glass beakers and bottles.

Asha sneaked a peek through the door, back toward the study. Could they get back to the dumbwaiter without the king spotting them?

The king commanded the wishes to descend from the ceiling. He had granted fourteen wishes last year. How dare the people of Rosas ask for more!

When he found the wishes of those who had questioned him in the courtyard, he toyed angrily with the bubbles. He tossed them into the air and swatted at them with his cape.

Asha watched, horrified. But she and her friends had to try to escape! They crawled along the wall toward the study, with Asha clutching Saba's wish in her hand.

King Magnifico was too worked up to notice. There was only one thing on his mind now: the forbidden spell book. The king strode back into the study just before Asha, Valentino, and Star reached the dumbwaiter.

They quickly hid beneath the desk. But as the king removed the book from the glass case and turned to read it, Asha, Star, and Valentino were mere inches away from the king's legs. They were trapped!

As the king opened the spell book, a sinister green magic swooped out and swirled around him. "Where was I?" he wondered aloud, flipping through the pages. "Oh yeah." As the king walked toward the window with the book, Asha, Star, and Valentino shrank back from view.

The king gazed out the window. There was a traitor in the town below. He willed whoever had conjured the light to come out and explain themselves. Then he whipped the curtains closed and turned back around—just as Asha, Star, and Valentino dove into the dumbwaiter.

As Asha struggled to close the door, Magnifico waved his arms, turning the floor a foreboding shade of green. Then the floor opened wide, revealing a circular staircase that descended into a secret chamber! With a final tug, Asha slid the dumbwaiter door down.

Caught up in his own glory, Magnifico gave an ominous laugh and started down the stairs with the forbidden book.

Later that evening, Sakina peered anxiously through the window of the cottage. Asha and Valentino had just returned from the castle with Saba's wish, and Sakina worried that the king and his guards might be close behind.

"I was not afraid, Sakina," Valentino boasted as he hopped from shelf to shelf overhead.

When Sakina turned away from the window, Star

hovered only inches from her face. "Oh. That's a little clo—" she said in surprise. "Oh. Hi. Hello."

Valentino suddenly lost his balance and toppled into Sakina's arms. "I fall because I am still learning," he said solemnly.

Sakina carried the goat toward the table, where Asha sat with Saba Sabino. Asha had wasted no time in returning her grandfather's wish. As the wish hovered before him, Saba stared at it with astonishment, his cheeks flushed pink.

"Saba, I know you said you didn't want to know a wish that could never be," said Asha. "But now you can *make* it be."

"It's so simple," he said, tears brimming in his eyes. "So pure."

"Asha," said Sakina, "I know you think you're doing a good thing, but—"

Sabino cut her off. "I should never have given Magnifico my wish. This," he said, gently cupping the bubble in his palms, "this belongs to me."

When he touched the bubble, the light and energy inside traveled straight to his heart. As Sabino reclaimed his wish, he laughed through his tears.

"Saba . . . ," said Sakina, seeing how vivacious Sabino suddenly appeared.

"This is everything," said Sabino, his eyes sparkling

with life. "Oh, Asha, I may never actually inspire anybody, but now at least I have the chance to try."

When Asha saw the wonder in Sakina's face, she took her mother's hands. "I'm going back for your wish next, Mame," she promised.

"Where's my lute?" Sabino asked suddenly. "Where's my lute? I must hold it."

Star found the wooden lute, and Saba took the stringed instrument gently into his hands. "Thank you, my sweet Star." Then he smiled at Asha. "Might as well get started, eh?"

Sabino softly strummed the lute, transported by its beautiful sound. As he began to sing, Asha and Sakina listened. Valentino curled up in Sakina's lap, and Star nestled happily onto Asha's shoulder. Sabino sang of wishes that were worth making, dreams that were worth dreaming.

When Star swayed with the music, Asha held out her hand. Star twirled around her hand as if they were dance partners. Sakina held Valentino's front hooves, moving them in time to the music, too, until . . .

Bam!

The front door burst open. King Magnifico's imposing figure filled the entryway, his eyes ablaze with fury. "That's right, Asha," he bellowed. "You've been turned in!"

Asha jumped to her feet in shock.

Star puffed up, too, ready to fight. But Valentino grabbed Star and hid them both in a wooden chest filled with yarn.

"Where is it?" the king growled. "Where is the star?"

Sabino stepped in front of Asha, determined to keep her safe. "There's nothing here for you!" he told the king.

When Magnifico flicked his hand, green magic easily pushed Sabino aside. "How did you do it?" the king raged at Asha. "What sorcery did you use?"

"I know no sorcery," Asha answered honestly.

"You're a liar," countered Magnifico. "You ripped a star from the sky and used it to steal from me!"

"The wishes don't belong to you!" Asha argued.

Sakina tried to pull her daughter away, but Asha wouldn't back down. "You were never going to grant my saba's wish. And he deserves to have it back! They all deserve—"

"I told you, *I* decide what they deserve!" the king spat. When he reached inside his cloak and stepped toward Asha, Sakina rushed forward.

"Please, Your Majesty," Sakina begged. "She made a mistake. She won't do it again."

"Oh, I know she won't," agreed the king. He pulled a wish bubble from inside his cloak. "Does this feel familiar, Sakina?"

Sakina touched her hand to her heart and then reached for the bubble. "My wish . . . ," she breathed.

"Yes, your wish that you gave to me to keep it safe," said the king in an ominous tone, "because we all know what happens to wishes out in this real world. They get *crushed.*" He closed his fingers tightly around Sakina's wish.

"No!" Asha whispered.

With a cruel smile, Magnifico crushed the bubble in his hand. Sakina cried out in grief, and her knees buckled.

"Mame!" cried Asha. She rushed to her mother's side.

"Sakina! No!" cried Sabino.

They watched in horror as Magnifico's hand began to glow with the light and energy of Sakina's wish. "What is this?" said the king. He pressed his hand to his heart and absorbed Sakina's wish, pulling its glow into his body with a satisfied shiver.

"What a gift!" he exclaimed. Instantly, the king radiated with renewed vitality. "All this time I've protected the wishes, not knowing the power they yield. I feel as if I can do anything!" He advanced menacingly toward Asha.

Just then, a ball of yarn bounced off Magnifico's head. Startled, the king turned to see Star hovering over the box of yarn. And Star looked angry.

"The star . . . ," murmured the king. "I must have it."

When the king lunged for Star, Asha saw her chance. She pulled down a bookcase to block Magnifico's path so that her family could escape. "Let's go!" she cried. "Now!"

Star burst through the door and spun around the guards, binding them with string. They toppled over, unable to move. "Hey! What is that?" cried the guards, confused. "Is that yarn?"

Valentino trotted out next, followed by Asha and Sabino supporting Sakina by each arm. "Hurry, hurry!" cried Sabino.

Valentino pleaded with the guards' horses. "From one domesticated animal to another, help us!"

The horses gave an obedient whinny and knelt before Asha and her family.

"Careful," said Asha as she helped Saba and Sakina onto one horse. Then she joined Valentino on the back of another.

"That's it, Sakina," Sabino urged. "Hold on!"

At the *snap* of the reins, the horses galloped after Star into the forest, leaving Magnifico far behind.

Chapter Eleven

Star's magic parted the trees and brush, clearing a path for the horses that carried Asha and her family to safety. But as the horses leaped down an embankment, nothing but water stretched out ahead.

"Oh no!" cried Valentino. "We've run out of land."

"There's a boat," Asha said, pointing toward the pebbled shore. "Hurry."

Star rushed ahead to inspect the rowboat as Asha slid off her horse. She helped Sabino and Sakina dismount, too. "Easy, easy," Sabino warned Sakina, who was still unsteady.

"We've got you," Asha reassured her mother.

Valentino released the horses back into the woods. "Go," the goat ordered gruffly. "Return to your stables. Play dumb."

As the horses trotted away, Valentino leaped onto the boat's bow. He could see a small island in the distance, silhouetted by the setting sun. “I say we head for the islet,” he said. “It’s closest. We can hide there.”

Saba and Asha helped Sakina into the rowboat and then pushed away from shore. When Star sprinkled the oars with magic, they rowed on their own, faster than human arms could. Asha sat close to Sakina. Her mother looked so small huddled against Sabino. Her usually smooth, beautiful face was etched with terrible sadness.

Asha took Sakina’s hand, feeling a rush of guilt. “Mame” was all she could say.

“My heart knows this feeling,” Sakina murmured. “This is grief.”

Even Star snuggled up to Sakina, trying to soothe her with its warm light.

“I didn’t mean for this to happen,” Asha said sadly.

“I know, baby,” said Sakina.

“I was foolish to think I could change anything,” said Asha. “I should never have wished.”

Star took Asha’s head and shook it side to side as if to say, “No! How could you say such a thing?”

“It’s true,” said Asha. “My wish has ruined everything for my family. And now everyone in Rosas is at risk because of me.”

Star gazed sadly at Asha, wishing there was a way to comfort her.

Then Sakina spoke, her voice still weak. “No,” she

said. "Everyone in Rosas is at risk because of Magnifico."

Asha glanced back at the castle looming over Rosas. Her gaze drifted toward the wishing tree—where she had made the wish that changed everything—and then back to the castle, where so many wishes were still imprisoned.

Realization flooded Asha's chest. Her wish hadn't only been about wanting more for her family. She had wanted *everyone* in Rosas to have their wishes back. She had to help them!

"Our dear Rosas," Sabino murmured. "Your father's heart would break for what we now know."

As Asha and Star locked eyes, Star's expression shifted. Star had a way of communicating with Asha without words.

"I know what you're thinking," said Asha, "because I'm thinking it, too."

"Which means I'm probably thinking it, too," said Valentino, not wanting to be left out. "All you need to do is spell it out."

Asha nodded at Star. "Okay," she said, jutting out her chin. She had to save the wishes, but first, she had to make sure her family was safe. She leaned toward her mother and grandfather. "I love you both very much," she said.

"What is going on?" asked Sabino, his voice sharp with worry.

Asha stood and pulled her thick hair into a ponytail. "When you get to the islet, stay hidden from view," she instructed her family.

"What are you doing?" asked Sakina.

"I have to stop him," Asha said simply.

"No!" said Sakina.

"It's too dangerous!" cried Sabino.

But Asha's mind was made up. "I started this," she said. "I have to finish it, for everyone." She gave them both a quick hug. Then, before they could stop her, she jumped into the chilly waves.

Sakina stared into the churning water. "Asha!" she cried.

"No!" Sabino called out.

"Catch me!" Valentino bleated as he jumped into the water after Asha.

Star planted kisses on Saba's and Sakina's cheeks and sprinkled more magic on the oars so they would continue to row. Then Star set off after Asha, zooming above the water.

Asha took long steady strokes with Valentino perched on her back. "This is perfect. I'll steer . . . ," said the goat. "To the left . . . left, left, left!"

Sakina and Sabino watched helplessly as Asha, Valentino, and Star swam back to shore. But the enchanted oars kept rowing the boat forward, toward the safety of the islet.

In the secret lair beneath the study, King Magnifico stood before a gnarled altar, bathed in the green glow of a torch. "To harness a star . . . a staff of such power, even the night will bow to my command," Magnifico read from the forbidden book. "Sounds good to me. Ha!"

Before him, the images on the pages seemed to come to life, showing him how to create the magical staff. A green glow swirled around Magnifico's hands, leading them in the ways of forbidden magic.

Magnifico read the ingredients of the spell aloud: "One branch of mountain ash, bathed in Tollens' potion. Molten iron for strength, copper for a strike! And most important, the power cast from the innocent hearts of three."

Above the king's head, three wish bubbles were held captive in snaking ribbons of green light. These were the wishes of the townspeople who had dared to question the king in the courtyard. The bubbles huddled together, quivering in fear.

"Innocent you may be, but grateful you are not," said the king, "as you dared question me and all that I do for you." He plucked a reluctant bubble from above and glowered at it, as if it were a naughty child about to be punished.

Inside the bubble, a mountain climber was conquering a steep mountain peak. But that wish was not to be. In a cottage across the kingdom, the owner of the wish was pouring tea for his wife.

Magnifico gripped the wish tightly. "It's your own fault you're here," he said with disdain. "You don't deserve to be granted."

The mountain climber inside the bubble cowered, shrinking away from the king.

"But through me," said Magnifico, "you may serve a greater purpose." Without warning, he squeezed his fist, crushing the wish.

The man in the cottage dropped his teacup, overcome by a terrible feeling.

His wife clasped his hand. "What is it, my love?" she asked.

"A despair like I've never known," uttered the man as tears filled his eyes.

In the secret lair, Magnifico absorbed the glowing energy of the wish into his heart. Then he grabbed the other two wish bubbles—one showing a woman captaining a great ship and the other showing a woman flying with the birds she loved. Without a second thought, he crushed the bubbles.

In the marketplace, the woman who wished to be a sea captain dropped her broom and clasped her mouth in horror. In the courtyard, the woman feeding her beloved birds sat down hard on the fountain's edge, her face masked by grief. "What is this heartbreak?" she murmured to a concerned passerby who knelt beside her.

While these citizens of Rosas wrestled with overwhelming sorrow, King Magnifico summoned the energy from the crushed wishes to form a pointy, mirrored staff, mighty enough to produce the most powerful magic Rosas had ever seen. "Yes! Yes! *Yes!*" he cried with glee.

He was so focused on the staff that he barely saw, reflected in the mirrors, a light glowing behind him. Queen Amaya had come down the stairs. She glanced around the secret lair in surprise and shock.

When the king whirled to face her, he grinned wickedly. "Amaya, darling, come!" he crooned. "You're just in time to meet my new toy!"

He slammed the staff against the ground, releasing a bolt of green magic. Amaya jumped backward, just out of the magic's reach.

"Now *that* is power," said Magnifico. "Am I glowing? I feel as if I am." He spun in a circle. The king's eyes and body surged with an evil green light.

Amaya saw the open book of forbidden magic behind him. "Mi rey, how could you?" she cried. "You know the ways of forbidden magic are—"

"Unappreciated," the king finished for her. "Much

like I am by my people. By that *girl*! She did this. She pulled a star from the sky so she could destroy everything I've built."

"Asha? No, she only wanted her family's wishes back," said the queen, trying to reason with the king.

Magnifico grabbed his staff and pointed it at Amaya's throat. "Do you side with the traitor?" he demanded to know.

"No, no," Amaya answered quickly, trying to hide her fear. "You know I would never side with a traitor of Rosas."

Magnifico, unconvinced, let the staff's tip creep closer to the queen.

She glanced warily at the staff's sharp point and forced a smile. "Please, mi rey, I have believed in you from the moment we met. We built this kingdom together. There is nothing more important than that, I assure you."

Magnifico studied her face and then smiled, slowly lowering his staff. "Wonderful!" he said with a celebratory spin. "Now let's go set the stage! I'm on the hunt!"

Magnifico swept up the stairs with his cape swirling behind him. Amaya stood alone in the shadowy lair, her heart filled with dread. Had the forbidden magic changed the king forever?

Chapter Twelve

Later that night, as trumpets sounded, a crowd of anxious citizens stood near the stage watching guards hang freshly painted WANTED posters. One poster featured a beautiful girl with long, dark braids, and the other showed a very expressive star.

At that moment, Asha herself was slipping through the crowd disguised in a cloak. Valentino trotted by her feet, and Star clung to the top of her head, both hidden from view. Every now and then, Star stroked her forehead reassuringly.

Valentino tried to comfort Asha, too. "You know, all of this is just a bump in the road," he said. "A gigantically humongous bump."

"Thank you," said Asha. She glanced up at Star, who was still rubbing her head. "Okay, enough, stop. We have to find Dahlia and the others!"

Onstage, a guard stood over the three townspeople

whose wishes had been destroyed. They sat grief-stricken, their shoulders slumped. "Look at these poor people!" declared the guard. "Asha stole and destroyed their wishes! She must pay!"

The crowd erupted with surprise.

"Asha?"

"Is it true?"

"She seemed so sweet."

Suddenly, Asha spotted the teens standing near the stage. They looked just as bewildered as the rest of the crowd.

"They say her family's gone missing," said Safi.

"I bet she killed them," offered Gabo, reveling in the drama of the moment.

Asha's throat tightened. How could Gabo think such awful things?

But Dahlia looked skeptical. "This whole thing feels wrong," she murmured.

Just as Asha approached the teens, a streak of green magic shot out from the curtains at the back of the stage. The streak morphed into a pair of sinister hands, poised to grab the townspeople below. As the citizens cowered in fright, Magnifico swaggered onto the stage. He waved his new staff, sucking the green magic back inside.

Magnifico gave a cruel laugh. "Ha! Your faces! It's okay. You're okay. It's just a play on light!"

Relieved, the crowd began to clap and cheer.

Behind Magnifico, Queen Amaya stepped cautiously onstage and took her seat. Asha saw the queen's furrowed brow and trembling hands. Star noticed, too. Then they heard a mouse chattering underfoot.

Asha and Star exchanged a look. Somehow, Star knew just what Asha was thinking. As Star set off to enlist the mouse's help, Asha whispered "Discreetly!" She held a finger to her lips.

Onstage, Magnifico reveled in the spotlight. "You are all probably wondering why you are here," he said. "Yes, there's a savage teenager running around with a star destroying wishes. But guess who bravely came forward and identified her?"

As the curtains parted again, a burly, ginger-haired boy stepped out. Asha sucked in her breath.

"Give a big cheer for Simon O'Donohue!" announced the king.

Dahlia and the other teens gasped.

"Simon?" Asha said softly. "No. . . ." How could her friend have betrayed her?

While the astonished crowd began to clap, Simon shielded his eyes from the bright lights. He walked slowly toward Magnifico, as if afraid to get too close.

"I know! I know!" said the king, quieting the crowd. He put his arm around Simon. "Tell me, I was just as surprised as you all. Our sleepy little Simon here. No need to be nervous, Simon. Be proud! Show us your joy!"

"Yay, Rosas," said Simon, attempting a smile.

Just then, the mouse that Star had enchanted with stardust scampered up the back of the queen's chair. "Your Majesty," it whispered in her ear.

Amaya gasped when she saw the mouse. "Oh my," she said in surprise.

"I know, a talking mouse, but don't panic," said the mouse. "I'm very clean, and I have an important message for you." The mouse cleared its throat and then recited Asha's message: " 'You once said generosity is the true essence of Rosas. I see your fear, but Rosas needs your help now. Love, Asha.' " The mouse added proudly, "The love part was my idea."

The queen's eyes widened. As cheers rang out for Simon, she scanned the crowd, searching for Asha.

"So, my dear Simon, are you ready to see your wish?" asked the king, pulling a wish bubble from beneath his cape. "To be the king's most valiant, courageous, and loyal knight!"

"Just not a loyal friend," spat Gabo.

"Such betrayal," muttered Bazeema, appearing so suddenly that Gabo jumped.

"Bazeema, you are making it hard to like you," he groaned.

Onstage, Magnifico sent the wish bubble swirling

around Simon. Then, using the powerful magic of his staff, he lifted the lumbering teen into the air. "It is my great pleasure," announced the king, "to grant you your heart's desire."

But instead of bathing Simon in hope and joy, the king's sinister green magic began to squeeze him. Choke him. Crush him! When Simon cried out in pain, whispers of fear rippled throughout the crowd.

When Simon dropped back down, he was encased in heavy armor. He landed on the stage in a fighting stance and then raised his sword into the air. "Long live the king!" Simon bellowed in a voice not quite his own.

"Isn't that wonderful," said Magnifico, pleased with his creation. "Tell us, Simon—"

"There are six more traitors in the crowd, sir!" Simon announced.

Asha whirled to face her friends, but they were already running, weaving their way through the crowd.

Simon slammed his sword down as he named them all: "Irresponsible teens: Dahlia, Gabo, Dario, Safi, Hal, and Bazeema."

The crowd gasped, searching for the teens. Asha caught a glimpse of Dario, the tallest one, disappearing around a corner. She raced after him, pulling her cloak around Valentino and Star.

Meanwhile, Magnifico put a hand on Simon's shoulder and called on the crowd for support. "Find them so they may pay for their betrayal," he ordered. "Find Asha so you may be rewarded. But most importantly, find me that star so I will have the power to grant all of your wishes!"

The crowd went wild, determined to hunt down the traitors—determined to have their wishes granted.

CHAPTER THIRTEEN

Bazeema led the teens around the corner. "Come on!" she urged. "Just a little farther."

Asha raced to catch up. But when she and Valentino rounded the corner, they came face to face with a wall. The teens had disappeared! Star popped out from Asha's cloak and spun around, confused.

"It's a dead end," said Asha.

"A dead end with unsanded mahogany," said Valentino, checking out a wooden pallet leaning against the wall. He rubbed his rear against the wood, scratching an itch. That's when the pallet gave way and fell backward. Valentino had discovered a secret passageway!

"Good find, Valentino!" Asha exclaimed.

"My butt found it," Valentino pointed out.

Asha led her friends through the passageway. A long tunnel stretched out ahead, curving to the right. And from somewhere nearby, Asha heard a familiar voice.

"So *this* is how you sneak around, Bazeema?"

Asha picked up her pace, following the sound of Gabo's grumpy voice.

Bazeema had led the teens to a hidden storage room lined with narrow windows. The windows let in filtered light, revealing a room decorated with pillows, baskets, decorative lights, and even a few of Bazeema's paintings.

Hal smiled at the cozy hangout. "Gotta love secret rooms!" she said brightly.

"This is my quiet place," Bazeema explained with a hint of pride.

Safi tried to fight off a sneeze. "Dust doesn't bother you?" he asked. *Achoo!*

"I like dust," said Bazeema. "We're safe here."

"We're not safe anywhere," Gabo grumbled. "We're fugitives, thanks to Asha."

Dahlia jumped to Asha's defense. "She said she just wanted her family to have their wishes back," she reminded Gabo.

"And you believed her?" he scoffed.

At that moment, Asha stepped into the secret room. "It's the truth, Gabo," she said calmly.

Safi, Gabo, Bazeema, and Hal ducked behind Dahlia, as if they feared Asha.

"Agghhh!" cried Hal.

"Hide!" added Bazeema.

"We're all gonna die!" hollered Gabo.

"Am I nervous smiling?" Hal muttered. "I am, aren't I?"

Bazeema nodded but didn't take her eyes off Asha.

"Oh, hey, Asha," said Dario, who was standing chest-deep in a giant basket. "We were just talking about you."

"Hey, Dario," said Asha, relieved that at least one of her friends was acting normal.

Then Dahlia stepped forward. She wanted to give Asha a chance to explain herself. "Please say you didn't destroy those people's wishes," Dahlia said.

"Of course I didn't," said Asha. How could Dahlia believe otherwise? "It was Magnifico."

"Likely story," spat Gabo, his arms crossed.

But Safi considered Asha's words. "The king was acting awfully . . ." Safi held back a sneeze. "Awfully . . ."

Bazeema pressed Safi's handkerchief to his nose and finished the thought for him. "Awful," she said.

Dahlia nodded. "Simon looked like he was in pain."

"Right before he squealed on us," added Gabo.

Achoo! Safi wiped his nose. "Are we just doomed now?" he asked with a sniffle.

"Not if we fight," said Asha in a somber voice. Beside her, Star's brow stiffened with determination.

"Ha!" said Dario, chuckling. Then he saw Asha's expression. "Oh, you're being serious."

Asha knew they had to fight. The king was dangerous. The wishes weren't safe! But how could she make her friends understand?

As she began telling them what she had seen, Star started closing the shutters. Valentino helped, too, leaping up to the highest windows.

But as the room grew dark, the teens were still afraid. "What is she doing?" they asked one another.

Asha tried to tell them that they had been deceived—that Magnifico was not the man they thought he was. But the teens backed away from her warily. Only Dahlia seemed to be listening.

Star, who saw Asha struggling to find words, flew behind a colorful bottle to light up the room in an ominous green glow. Asha immediately understood: she could *show* her friends what she had seen. She stacked objects around the room to create shadows on the wall. With Star's help, Asha told a story with shadows to show her friends Magnifico's true colors, how evil he had become. If they didn't fight back, who would stop the king?

One by one, Asha's friends began to believe. Dahlia was the first to stand beside Asha. Sunny Hal and skeptical Gabo were prepared to fight. Even shy Bazeema found her voice, ready to stand up against the king. They didn't know if they would win, but they had to try. How could they not, knowing what they had learned?

As the teens began planning a revolution, the door

to the hidden room flew open. Queen Amaya stood before them. For a moment, the teens froze. Would she hand them over to the king?

Then Amaya and Asha locked eyes, and Asha knew they could trust the queen. She, too, was ready to fight the king who valued his crown and power above all else.

Star hovered near the queen, as fascinated by her as she was with it. "Hi," said Amaya. "Goodness . . ."

"This is Star," said Asha, introducing them.

Queen Amaya gazed at Star, entranced. "You are extraordinary," she murmured.

Star blushed and waved, humbly dismissing the compliment.

Then worry flickered across Amaya's face. "You need to know, Magnifico's powers have only grown, in the most dangerous way," she warned Asha. "He is intent on capturing Star." She gazed at Star, her expression grave. "He wants to take all your energy for himself."

Asha felt a trickle of fear. She turned to Star in dread.

"Then Star needs to leave," said Gabo, "like right now."

Star zoomed toward Gabo, reached out its limbs, and shook Gabo's head *no.*

"Star won't go until those wishes are free," Asha explained with a heavy sigh.

Star, who still hovered beside Gabo, nodded.

But Asha couldn't bear the thought of anything happening to Star. She drew her little friend close. "I'll make sure Magnifico doesn't get anywhere near you," she promised.

"Does that mean you have a plan?" Hal asked hopefully.

Asha hesitated a moment too long.

"I knew it," said Gabo, exasperated. "She doesn't have a plan. We're doomed."

Just then, Valentino toppled from his perch. But Asha was there, ready to catch him—just as she would always be there, ready to protect all her friends. "Of course I have a plan," she said to Gabo.

And this time, he believed her.

Later that night, Magnifico stood in his secret lair with five wish bubbles quivering above him.

The king raised his hand, summoning them downward. "You are the most ambitious wishes," he said in a menacing voice. "You know what that means . . ."

He waved his sharp staff, swirling the wishes round and round. Then he poked at them one by one.

"You will never be granted," said the king. When he poked the first bubble, it shrank back. "You will never be granted," he continued, prodding another. "You will never be granted . . . so I figure, no point in wasting your energy when you can be of use to me."

As Magnifico pointed his staff at another wish, Amaya came down the stairs. "Mi rey! Asha and Star have been spotted in the forest!" she announced, trying to sound cheery. The king had to believe that she still supported him.

The king turned, his eyes glowing green. "Is that so?" he said. "How fortunate."

"Shall we gather the citizens so they can see you capture her?" asked Amaya.

"Oh, we've been gathering them a lot lately, don't you think?" countered Magnifico. He tapped the sharp tip of his staff thoughtfully.

"I, um . . ." Amaya struggled for words. Once the wishes were freed, the citizens of Rosas *had* to be present to reclaim them. It was part of Asha's plan!

"I'm kidding!" said the king. He shoved the staff toward her playfully. "Sound the trumpets, Amaya! I'll bring back the girl *and* the star!"

King Magnifico rushed past Amaya, his cape billowing behind him. As soon as he was gone, Amaya tiptoed up the stairs to the study. She peeked out from the staircase to make sure the coast was clear and then hurried toward the dumbwaiter.

"Okay, we must work quickly," she whispered as she

slid open the door. Valentino and the teens were all crammed inside.

"And quietly!" Valentino bleated loudly. He dropped his voice back down to a whisper. "Sorry. Goats have poor volume control."

Then he scrambled out, ready to put Asha's plan into action.

From the forest's edge, Asha heard trumpets calling the citizens of Rosas together. She knew that at any moment, Magnifico would begin making his way through the woods to find her—and Star.

Asha's stomach ached at the thought of anything happening to Star. "Okay," she said to Star, "I'm going to keep him far away from you. As soon as Magnifico leaves the castle, you're safe to join the others. Once the wishes are free, return them to the people and then . . ." She fought back the emotion rising in her chest. "You must return to the sky."

Star threw all five limbs around Asha's face, hugging tightly so that she would stop talking.

"I know," said Asha, her voice muffled. "But it's the only way."

She tried to pry Star off her face but couldn't. Then they heard the castle gate opening in the distance. "That's the gate, Star," she said. "Star!"

Star let go, but its usually bright face was clouded with worry.

"It'll be okay," Asha promised. "He won't harm me as long as he thinks I'm the only way he can get to you."

Star, who didn't look convinced, began searching the forest for something—anything—that might help Asha defend herself. Finally, Star grabbed a stick from the ground and sprinkled stardust on its tip.

"What are you doing?" she asked.

Star handed Asha the stick and gestured for her to point and flick it, like a wand. When she did, she accidentally cast a spell on a nearby apple tree! A red apple swelled to the size of a hay bale and plunked to the ground.

"Ha! Oops. I'm sorry. It's magic," said Asha, realizing now the gift Star had given her. "Thank you!"

When a horse whinnied nearby, Asha steeled herself. The king was getting closer. "I'll draw him this way," she said to Star. "You have to go, *now.*"

Star gave her one more loving look, as if in awe of the courageous fighter she had become.

"I know, you're proud of me," said Asha. "I'm proud of us."

Star gave a reluctant wave and then zipped toward the castle, where the teens and Queen Amaya were already proceeding with their part of the plan. All

Asha had to do now was lead the king as far away from Star and the wishes as possible.

She tried again with the wand, cautiously waving her arm. The wand sent a blast of sparkling magic into the air. "Wow, that worked," Asha murmured in surprise. Surely the king would see the magic filling the sky. But would it be enough to lure him this way?

The king, who was out searching for Asha and Star on horseback, glanced up in surprise at the fireworks. "There you are," he cried, his face contorting into a wicked smile. "Challenge accepted!"

He steered his horse toward the display of magic, ready to hunt down the girl who dared challenge his power—and to seize that magical star.

Chapter Fourteen

Back in the observatory, the teens stared upward, entranced by the beautiful wishes. Valentino leaped onto a bookshelf to get closer, climbing higher and higher toward the domed roof.

"So beautiful," murmured Bazeema.

"Untouched by any allergens," said Safi.

"I've never felt so wonderful," said Hal, breathing it all in.

Even Gabo seemed impressed by the wishes. "I have nothing bad to say," he said, sounding surprised by himself.

Dario was moved to poetry. "Through the heart we understand the world," he said eloquently.

The teens whirled toward him, shocked. Had Dario just said something wise?

"Dario, those might be the greatest words you've ever . . . ," Hal began.

But Dario had already moved on. "Oh, look, hot drinks!" he said, hurrying toward the king's vats of boiling potions.

Bazeema rushed after him. "Dario, no!" she cried. "Those are dangerous chemicals."

Just then, Star swooped into the observatory.

"Well, took you long enough," said Gabo, back to his snarky self.

At the sight of Star, Hal kicked into action. "This is it, everyone," she said. "First, we open the roof, and then Star returns the wishes."

Safi gazed around the room. "The queen said look for giant pulleys," he reminded the teens. But where were they?

"Look up!" bleated Valentino.

They followed his gaze toward a small circular ledge just below the domed ceiling. From there, they could reach the pulleys that opened the panels in the roof. But how would they ever reach the ledge?

"Ahh! No! No. No," Gabo protested. "I hate heights."

"Don't worry," Valentino assured him. "You're with me. I've been preparing for this summit my entire life." But as he puffed out his chest, he suddenly fell, landing awkwardly in Gabo's arms. "It's fine," said Valentino with a sigh. "With each fall, we learn to climb higher."

He leaped out of Gabo's arms and began to climb

again, bounding from one shelf to the next. But Gabo wouldn't follow.

"Nope. No way," said Gabo. Then he saw Star swirling stardust around the room. "Whoa!"

Thanks to Star's magic, the king's desk began to gallop across the floor, with chairs and tables trotting close behind. The furniture scooped the teens off the ground and then stacked together, lifting them upward.

"And away we go!" cried Hal with glee.

Valentino called out to the teens as he climbed the wall nearby. "Just grip with your hooves and don't look down!" he advised. Finally, he was an expert in *something*!

Hidden behind a tree trunk, Asha heard hoofbeats. Magnifico was getting closer, and she was ready. She dashed behind a clump of bushes. Then she raised her wand and shot a streak of magic in the opposite direction, hoping to mislead the king.

Instead, her magic bounced off a tree and zapped back, straight toward the bushes in front of her! The bushes suddenly waddled away, revealing Asha's hiding place—just as the king rode into view.

Asha took off running, but she was no match for Magnifico's horse. The king galloped after her in pursuit of his prize. It was only a matter of time now. . .

In the king's secret lair, Queen Amaya and Dahlia stood before the pages of the forbidden book.

"I've read all the other spell books in his library," Amaya confessed.

Dahlia's eyes widened. "There are thousands!" she said.

Amaya nodded. "A queen must be prepared. I understand how to bind simple spells, if needed, but not magic such as this."

She pulled a small potion bottle from her pocket. "Obsidian oil for protection from the pages," she explained, offering the oil to Dahlia. "Cover your hands with it before you touch the book."

Then Amaya carefully opened the book. "Look for anything on how to break his staff, bind his magic, or, at the very least, break the hold this horrible magic has on him," she said.

Together, she and Dahlia skimmed the contents of the book. Would they be able to find the spell they were looking for—and stop the king?

Asha ran for her life, with Magnifico close behind. When she came upon a wheeled cart, she jumped in. As the cart careened wildly down a hill, Asha tried to blast magic at Magnifico with her wand. But the streak of magic hit a patch of mushrooms instead, turning them into butterflies.

Asha tried again, carefully aiming her wand. But her magic missed its mark once more. A tree behind her now wore a frilly pink dress!

"I don't get you at all," Asha grumbled at the wand. Then she apologized to the dress-wearing tree. "I'm sorry!"

"But I love it!" said the tree, admiring itself. "Now, *this* is how you dress a tree!" As if to say thank you, the tree swung out a limb, blocking Magnifico's path. *Smack!*

The king hit his head against the branch. "Ouch! Aww! Grrrr . . . ," he grumbled. But he kept riding.

It would take more than an enchanted tree to stop Magnifico.

Back in the observatory, the teens had finally reached the ledge near the ceiling. They stationed themselves at the pulleys, readying themselves to open the panels in the roof and free the wishes. But when they yanked the ropes, nothing happened.

"It won't move!" said Safi. Beside him, Star was tangled up in the rope.

Even optimistic Hal grew frustrated. "I'm trying my hardest!" she cried.

Then Gabo noticed that Dario was moving the ropes in the opposite direction instead of pulling them. "Dario!" he exclaimed. "It's called a pulley for a reason!"

Dario looked down at the rope in his hand. "Oh, okay," he said. "Thanks." He started to pull, but it didn't help. The roof stayed closed.

Valentino leaped onto Gabo's head for a better view. "Come on," said the goat. "It's as obvious as my baby beard. You must pull *together.* On my count: One . . . two . . . nine zillyboo . . . twenty alphabet . . ."

Gabo's face scrunched up with confusion. "Wait, what?"

"I forgot," said Valentino sadly. "Goats can't count."

"Now!" cried Hal, who was more than ready.

The teens all pulled at the same time and . . . the six hexagonal panels in the observatory roof began to creak open.

"That's it," Valentino bleated joyfully. "Give it all you've got!"

The roof panels revealed a glimpse of the night sky. But they were too heavy for the teens to pull all the way open. As the ropes slipped from their hands, the panels slammed back shut.

The teens watched in despair. Now what?

In the secret lair, Dahlia and Amaya had skimmed enough of the forbidden book to be worried—very worried.

"This reads like a recipe book for the foul and the savage," declared Dahlia, who had read her share of recipe books.

Amaya began to pace, recalling what they had read. "He's become practically untouchable," she said of the king. "No metal can break his staff. No spell can bind his magic."

"No one can bring him back from this," said Dahlia. She read a passage from the book out loud: "Embrace that which is forbidden but once, and you surrender to it for eternity."

Amaya's shoulders slumped. "I warned him," she whispered.

"I'm sorry," said Dahlia.

Amaya and Dahlia locked eyes. It was too late to rescue the king from himself. But if their plan to free the wishes worked, then maybe they could still save Rosas.

Back in the forest, Magnifico was closing in on Asha. And her cart was heading straight for an antlered buck!

Asha waved frantically at the deer. "I can't turn!" she cried. "I can't turn!"

But the buck was frozen in fear. "Stop staring, stop staring," the buck pleaded with itself. "I can't stop staring!"

Finally, Asha held up her wand. "Okay, work for me," she begged the wand. "Please."

With a wave of the wand, Asha blasted the cart with magic. Just in time, its wheels turned to legs. Instead of crashing into the buck, the cart ran *around* it—missing the animal by mere inches. Then with its newly minted legs, the cart climbed straight up the wall of a nearby cliff. Asha gripped the edges of the cart for dear life.

Asha's magic wasn't perfect, but maybe it would be enough to escape King Magnifico. "Whatever gets it done," Asha murmured as the cart continued to climb the rocky wall, going up, up, up. . . .

In the observatory, the exhausted teens strained on the ropes of the pulley, willing the roof panels to open back up.

"Why isn't this working?" cried Safi.

"We need more weight!" declared Gabo.

Valentino, who was still perched on Gabo's head,

looked over the railing of the ledge. "Well, you know what they say," he said. "It's not falling if you jump."

Gabo peered at the floor far below and shuddered. But there was no other choice. "Oh, what the heck!" he cried. "For Rosas!"

Together, Gabo and Valentino jumped over the railing, still holding the rope.

Hal and Safi watched them go, and then urged the others to follow their lead. "Jump! Jump!"

Gripping their ropes tightly, the teens leaped over the railing. They rode the ropes to the floor, all their weight pulling downward. And this time, it was enough to lift the roof panels wide open! The teens whooped and hollered as they landed safely on the observatory floor.

Star soared toward the opening in the roof, and the wish bubbles floated up and out of the observatory, toward the safety of the starry sky.

"Look at that," said Gabo in wonder. "Something worked out."

In the courtyard below, townspeople watched the glowing wish bubbles spilling out through the roof. As they rose skyward, people murmured with confusion. "Are those our wishes? They must be. What is this feeling?"

Sakina and Sabino watched, too, from the islet

beyond Rosas. They stood, arms entwined, staring at the magical sight.

"The wishes," Sabino realized. "She did it, Sakina!"

"Our girl," Sakina whispered with pride.

Then Sabino made a decision. "Come on." He shuffled toward the boat, climbed inside, and reached for the oars.

Sakina climbed in after him. "Saba," she said, "you're one hundred years old."

"So? My will is strong," Sabino pointed out. But when he tried to lift the oars, he struggled. "But your arms are stronger, my dear," he admitted, allowing Sakina to take the oars.

"Thank you," said Sakina. With renewed energy, she began to row back toward the shores of Rosas.

Chapter Fifteen

As Asha's enchanted cart raced through a clearing in the woods, something caught her eye in the distant sky. It was a glowing stream of wish bubbles, rising from the observatory roof! And, in their midst, Star shone bright.

"They did it!" cried Asha joyfully.

But Magnifico had found another path toward Asha, riding so close now that his horse rammed the cart she was riding in. As Asha tumbled out, her wand skittered across the ground.

The king's horse stopped just short of trampling her. Magnifico jumped off the horse and stepped on the wand, snapping it in half with a cruel laugh.

"No!" Asha cried.

Then the king stood over Asha, glaring down.

Even from her precarious position, Asha was defiant. "It's over, Magnifico," she said. "You're too late."

The king glanced back at the castle. Then a green

glow began to envelop him. "Asha . . . ," he said, sounding more sinister than ever.

When the green cloud dissipated, it wasn't Magnifico standing before her. It was Simon! "Magnifico's *never* too late," said Simon in a mocking voice.

"Simon? No," Asha gasped, staring up at the armored teen. If Simon was here, that meant the king . . . was still at the castle! "Star," Asha uttered. Was her little friend in danger? She had to do something!

With all the strength she could muster, Asha leaped to her feet and gave Simon a shove. But he didn't budge. He was too big!

"Ha," snarked Simon. "You really think you can—"

Just then, a bear lumbered into the clearing and tackled Simon from the side. Together, they tumbled down a ravine. "Ah!" cried Simon.

In seconds, Asha had mounted Simon's horse and began galloping back toward the castle. "Thanks, John!" she called over her shoulder.

"Anytime, Asha!" boomed the bear's voice from deep within the ravine.

Simon landed on his back. His suit of armor weighed him down as he scrambled backward away from the bear. "Ah, please don't hurt me," Simon pleaded as the bear rose to its feet.

"It's not me you should be afraid of," replied the bear, with a friendly growl.

At that moment, enchanted rabbits emerged from the thicket and surrounded Simon.

"Boom!" said a rabbit as it hopped closer to Simon. "Did we just blow your mind?"

Simon gasped. If these rabbits could talk, what else were they capable of? "Ah!" he cried, flailing his limbs.

Queen Amaya followed the teens into the courtyard to join the excited citizens of Rosas. High above, Star twirled happily among the wishes as it led them up and out of the observatory.

"I always say, never lose hope," said Gabo with newfound optimism.

But the reunion of wishes with wishers wasn't meant to be.

From the observatory below, an electric green light shot upward and wrapped itself around Star and the wishes. The teens gasped in horror.

"Star!" cried Dahlia.

"Oh no!" gasped Bazeema.

Beneath the open roof, Magnifico stood at the center of the wish chamber, his sinister staff raised high. "Surprise," he said with delight.

Star struggled against the green light snaking from the king's staff but couldn't escape!

When the king waved his free hand toward the floor, the entire platform rose, lifting the king skyward.

Even from the forest, Asha could see the evil green magic shooting from the observatory roof, with Star's golden light trapped within. "Star!" she cried, urging the horse to gallop faster.

In the courtyard, the crowd murmured in confusion. What was happening to their wishes—and to the bright star that had freed them? The teens huddled together anxiously.

"Please. No," Queen Amaya pleaded as Magnifico rose through the roof of the observatory. Bathed in a green glow, the king had never looked more powerful.

"Good evening, Rosas!" the king greeted his subjects. But his voice couldn't reach them from such a great height. "Let's try that again," said the king. He waved his hand and rippled the air with magic, which amplified his voice. "Good evening, Rosas!"

The townspeople spun around, overwhelmed by the voice that seemed to come from all directions.

Then Magnifico swirled his staff overhead, causing the wish bubbles—and Star—to swirl, too. "Wow, the stars are really out tonight!" joked Magnifico. "That was mean, I know. But what can I say? I really, really, *really* don't like being betrayed!"

From the midst of the spinning wishes, Star tried to gather them close—to keep the wishes safe.

Brave Amaya stepped forward and called out to the king. "It is *you* who betrays your people!"

"Nope, nope," said the king. "I've had enough of you!" He aimed his staff and blasted her with green magic.

Amaya gasped in pain and stumbled backward. The teens caught her in their arms.

"No!" cried Dahlia.

While the king was distracted with Amaya, Star charged at the edges of the green magic that held it and the wishes captive.

"I have all I need right here!" the king continued, gesturing toward Star.

Just then, Star managed to push one of the wishes free from the green magic.

"Wait! What's this?" asked the king. "A rogue wish?" He summoned the wish to him. Then Magnifico squeezed his fist, crushing the wish and absorbing its energy.

A woman in the courtyard below cried out in anguish as her wish was destroyed. Her family gathered round her.

Star shrank back in horror.

"You shouldn't have done that, little star," said Magnifico in a singsong voice. "The wishes aren't yours to free. They are mine." He gazed at the wishes still trapped overhead. "That's right. Now bow down to your king!" he commanded, slamming his staff downward.

The wishes plunged from the sky like lead weights and clunked onto the platform. Below, the townspeople huddled together in terror. Star hovered nearby, so deflated and sad that the little orb didn't realize that it was now free of the evil magic.

Asha, who had finally reached the castle, slid off her horse. "Star!" she cried. "Get away from there!"

When Magnifico saw Asha, he smiled wickedly and raised his staff, ensnaring Star once more with a bolt of green light. At the same time, the king waved his hand toward Asha. A shaft of green light snaked around her body, holding her prisoner.

"Asha!" cried the teens.

Lowering his staff, the king brought Star closer, until they were face to face. But instead of being frightened, Star stared at the king defiantly.

"You really are spectacular," said the king. "But let me ask you something. Where were you when *I* needed you? Why did it take *her*"—he tugged on the magical green rope, yanking Asha up onto his platform—"for us to meet?"

With green energy flying from both his staff and his free hand, the king stood between his two prisoners. "Well, hello, Asha!" he said with false charm. "So glad you could join us. I hoped you might answer a very important question for us all."

Asha looked desperately at Star, helpless against Magnifico's strength.

"Tell me," the king continued, tightening the grip of his magic, "how's the whole *taking your wish into your own hands* working out for you?" But Asha was in too much pain to answer.

"What's that?" mocked the king. "Sure, I'd be happy to answer for you." He slammed the bottom of his staff on the platform, yanking Star downward. In an instant, Star was sucked straight into the diamond tip of the staff! A flash of green light radiated in all directions, filling the sky.

"No!" Asha cried. She landed with a sickening thud on the platform near the king. Devastated by the loss of Star, she clutched her heart.

But the king wasn't finished yet. Using his magic, he angled every mirrored surface in the kingdom so that they all reflected his image. Then he leaned menacingly over Asha. "It hurts, doesn't it?" he said. "It really, really hurts."

As Asha began to sob, wracked with grief, the king savored her pain—and his own power. "But *I* feel great," he said. "And that's all that matters."

Queen Amaya, still weak from the king's blow, held

tight to Dahlia and Hal. "We have to help her," Amaya pleaded with the teens.

Desperate to save their friend, the teens helped Amaya toward the castle. But at the king's command, glowing green vines snaked across the entrances and sealed the doors shut.

Magnifico began gleefully whacking the wishes with his staff, as if he were playing a game. "Oh, that sound is so satisfying, isn't it?" exclaimed the king. "Got some good distance on that one." The wishes rolled heavily and knocked into one another.

As a wish rolled past Asha, she lifted her head. "Stop," she begged. "Please. What about your people? You promised to protect their wishes at all costs."

Magnifico paused, as if remembering. "I did say that, didn't I?"

Then he glanced down at the wishes and sighed. "I should thank you, Asha," he said. "If you hadn't challenged me, I would still think I needed everyone's trust and that the closest I could get to happiness was being near their wishes. I never would have realized that I could just *take* what I wanted for myself!"

He laughed and looked down at the crowd, his reflection looming large from every direction. "That's right," he announced. "I don't need any of you anymore!"

Asha forced herself to stand. If the king didn't need

the people of Rosas, what might he do to them? With everything she had, Asha rushed at Magnifico. She grabbed the sharp staff, trying to wrestle it away. But he easily shoved her backward. Furious that he hadn't broken her will, he blasted her again with magic.

Asha cried out in pain. As Sakina and Sabino climbed out of the boat at the harbor, they saw Asha's anguished face reflected in the mirrors Magnifico had created.

"Asha! No!" Sabino cried.

"Hurry!" said Sakina, urging him toward the kingdom.

Asha rolled onto her back and looked up at the stars twinkling overhead. She reached her hand toward the stars, wondering if she could make one more wish.

"Oh no you don't!" Magnifico barked. "There will be no wishing on stars ever again!" With a swoop of his staff, the king conjured up a black cloud that spread throughout the sky, blocking the stars. "In fact, there will be no more hope, no more dreams, and no escape."

As darkness fell, Asha's hopes did, too. No more stars? What would become of Rosas?

CHAPTER SIXTEEN

Rosas fell into darkness, except for the king himself—and his reflection in the mirrors. At the king's command, green coils of light snaked across the courtyard and wrapped around the ankles of the people below. Amaya and the teens were soon trapped in its tentacles. Sabino, Sakina, and Valentino were, too! Terrified cries rose from the crowd.

"No chance to rise up," bellowed the king. "No one to tell any tales. No one to challenge me ever again!"

Asha looked down at her friends and family struggling to break free from the forbidden magic. "I'm so sorry . . . ," she cried.

"Aw," mocked the king. "Did you hear that, folks? She's sorry. That's right, because of her, you all have had to lose everything."

As the townspeople clung to one another, Asha's hand covered her heart, which was breaking. Then she remembered something. She willed herself to sit up and face Magnifico, even in her weakened state.

"No. You're wrong," she said simply. "You can rip our dreams from our hearts . . . destroy them before our eyes. But you can't take from us what we are—"

"YOU . . . ARE . . . *NOTHING*!" the king roared. He blasted her again and sent her tumbling to the edge of the platform. She curled up in a tight ball of pain. But as she looked down at the crowd, she locked eyes with Dahlia.

"We . . . are . . . stars," Asha said weakly, remembering what the forest creatures had taught her. If every living thing was made of stardust, then they could use that power to fight.

Asha was in so much pain, she couldn't stand. But she reached out a single hand toward Dahlia and summoned all her strength. Then, in a weak but clear voice, Asha began to sing.

Magnifico, furious now, struck her with another bolt of magic—prepared to kill the girl who still defied him.

Asha could barely breathe, but she forced herself to go on, to keep singing. She told her loved ones below that they were *all* stars.

"You really need to learn to give up," the king scoffed, shaking his head at the foolish girl. But he couldn't see that her heart had begun to glow.

From the courtyard below, Dahlia saw the radiant

white light of Asha's heart in the mirrors surrounding the courtyard, and she began to understand.

Asha took a breath and continued to sing, urging the people of Rosas to stand beside her, reminding them that they could use the stardust that connected them to defeat Magnifico. As Asha sang, the light of her heart grew stronger.

Magnifico saw it now, too. Enraged, he blasted Asha with his staff one last time. When her limp body fell silent and the light in her heart vanished, the king smiled, satisfied that he had won, until . . .

Dahlia began to sing. She sang for Asha, who couldn't. And as she did, Dahlia's heart glowed bright.

Magnifico struck Dahlia with magic, but the glow from her heart somehow deflected it. Instead of hitting Dahlia, it struck an arch overhead, which began to crumble. The teens pulled Dahlia out of the way of the falling bricks.

When Amaya saw the light and Dahlia's courage, she joined in the song. So did Valentino and the rest of the teens. As they began to sing, their hearts radiated light.

Magnifico tried again to destroy the teens below, but the light from their hearts deflected his magic. The loving white glow reflected back at him from a mirror, sending him stumbling backward. "Argh!"

Sakina and Sabino began to sing, too, the glow from

their hearts blinding the king. His magic missed its mark again and hit a wall, which crumbled.

Asha's friends sang louder, their light growing stronger. As weak as Asha was, she smiled at the sound of their voices.

In the radiant light rising from the courtyard, the king's staff trembled in his hands. "No . . . no! No!" the king cried. "Stop!" He slammed the bottom of the staff against the platform, sending more blasts of green light throughout the kingdom. He couldn't give up control. He *wouldn't.*

The king's magic crumbled brick and stone, but the citizens of Rosas were safe, protected by their shining hearts. As they raised their voices in song, that glowing light mingled and morphed into a single beam. In a sudden burst, it shot up toward the platform, straight toward the mirrored tip of Magnifico's staff.

Asha felt the light's energy. Magnifico, who was still fighting for control of his staff, felt it, too. The staff suddenly broke free from his grip, as if Star—who was trapped inside—had taken control.

Asha pushed herself up to her hands and knees and began to sing again, her voice ringing out over Rosas. The people below joined hands and sang together as one. And in the face of the bright light emanating from their hearts, the green vines holding the townspeople captive began to wither.

Gaining strength, Asha rose to her feet. Magnifico's staff rose, too, out of the king's reach. He leaped, trying to get ahold of it. But all around him, the wishes that had fallen to the platform stirred and floated into the air.

The king's chest heaved, and the wishes he had crushed and absorbed sprang free from his body. "No! Those are *my* wishes!" he cried.

But they weren't his any longer. The wishes, now free, joined the other bubbles hovering overhead.

Asha and the crowd below sang louder, knowing now that if they stood together, they could defeat the king. The light of their hearts glowed like a sea of stars.

Bolstered by song, Star's magical light suddenly shot free from Magnifico's staff. A beam of golden light cut through the black sky. The cloud blocking the stars vanished, and the stars returned. Then Star zoomed out of the king's staff in a brilliant blast.

Just as quickly, the staff began to swallow the king into its mirrored diamond tip. His once handsome face, now distorted, twisted in fear and agony as . . . *sloop*! He was sucked entirely into the staff's finial, his shrieking voice growing distant.

As the staff crashed to the ground far below, the last remnants of green magic disintegrated. The vines that snaked around the castle crumbled away.

The crowd cheered. "We did it!" the teens cried. "We're free! Magnifico's gone!"

Overhead, Star swirled around the wish bubbles, sending them floating gently down to their rightful owners. Then Star flew toward Asha, bombarding her with hugs and stardust.

"Star!" she cried, laughing with joy.

As townspeople reached up to retrieve their wishes, a brilliant warmth settled over the crowd. The people of Rosas reclaimed their wishes and their hearts glowed with contentment.

Asha and Star rushed from the castle just in time to see Sakina's wish bubble floating toward her.

"Oh, my beautiful wish," crooned Sakina. She caught the wish in her cupped hands, her face bathed in its light.

Asha could barely contain her own joy. She hugged her mother and Sabino tight.

"My baby!" Sakina cried.

"Asha!" said Sabino.

Star joined the hug, too.

"I'm so happy," cried Hal as the teens joined the group hug.

At the sound of clanking armor, Asha pulled away. She turned to see Simon trudging into the courtyard. As the green magic faded, his armor began to crumble. Chunks fell to the ground, quickly turning to dust.

"Well, look who finally woke up," said Valentino gruffly as he glared at him.

Asha saw by Simon's sorry expression that it was the old Simon—no longer the king's spellbound knight.

"Asha, I'm sorry," he said, lowering his eyes. "I'm so sorry. I don't expect you to forgive me. I was just scared I'd have to live without, well, all of me. . . . And I wanted so badly to believe in him." Simon's face flushed in shame.

"So did I," said Queen Amaya, who stood nearby.

"We all did," Asha admitted.

Simon gave her a grateful smile.

Then Gabo leaned toward Simon and said, "Never trust a handsome face." He smirked and added, "That's why I hang out with you guys."

For the first time in a long time, Asha and her friends—*all* of her friends—were back together.

In the midst of the celebration, Queen Amaya, Asha, and her friends heard a familiar voice, menacing though muffled. Amaya's eyes widened.

"Hello?!" the quiet voice called, demanding attention. "Hello! This is your king!"

Amaya tracked the voice to the king's broken staff, which lay shattered on the ground. The mirrored finial was still intact, and Magnifico was trapped inside!

Amaya gasped.

From his mirrored prison, Magnifico spotted the

queen. "Amaya, thank goodness!" he cried. "Do you see what they have done to me?"

"Well, you do love mirrors," said Amaya, "so . . ."

Asha, Dahlia, and Valentino stepped up behind Amaya. The townspeople nearby clustered around the queen, too, watching.

"That is not funny. Get me out of here at once," the king commanded.

"No," said Amaya without a moment's hesitation.

"What?" squawked the king. "After everything I've done for you, for Rosas, this is the thanks I get?"

Amaya picked up the mirror and looked into Magnifico's eyes. "*This* is the thanks you deserve," she replied.

The queen turned to a guard standing nearby and handed him the mirror. "Hang it on the wall," she instructed him. "In the dungeon."

"Wait, what?" Magnifico shrieked. "I won't stand for this!" As the guard took the mirror away, the king could still be heard shouting, "Amaya! Amaya! No! The dungeon smells!"

The crowd behind the queen began to cheer.

"Long live the queen!" declared Asha.

"Long live the queen!" echoed Dahlia.

EPILOGUE

Now that the king was gone, Rosas could become a true kingdom of wishes. As dawn broke and darkness fell away, Asha and Star walked through the city, reveling in all the wishes that could finally come true.

They passed the woman with the ponytail talking with her parents.

"A ship's captain?" exclaimed her mother. "But you're terrified of water."

"Ha, I know!" laughed the woman. "But I think I'm ready to tackle my fear." She pulled her parents into a joyful hug.

Then Asha and Star passed the woman who wished to fly like a bird. "Flying, imagine that," she said aloud. She laughed, perplexed by her wish.

The man beside her was folding paper. "Well, I want to be an inventor," he said, "so how about we work together?" He handed her the paper, which now sported two folded wings, and her face lit up with hope and possibility.

As the paper airplane soared past Asha, she heard a familiar voice from above. "The key to climbing," said her favorite goat, "is confidence!"

Valentino stood on a mountain of rubble with the man who wished to be a mountain climber. He wobbled beside Valentino, looking very nervous.

"Ropes help, too," admitted Valentino.

Asha laughed and scooped Valentino into her arms before making her way toward Sakina, who was listening to Saba play his lute. Townspeople surrounded him, dancing and laughing. Even Queen Amaya sashayed to the music!

Asha beamed as she watched the celebration. "This is more than I could have ever dreamed possible," she told Star, her voice filled with awe.

Valentino nodded in agreement. "I'm starting to think a dream is a wish your heart makes," he added.

Star perked up with an idea, zipping off into the forest.

"Wait," said Asha, looking for Star. "Where'd you go?"

Star reappeared moments later holding the damaged wand.

"I know," said Asha, her face falling at the sight. "I'm sorry I broke it."

Star mended the wand in a flash with a bit of stardust, then gave it an extra dose to make it stronger and more beautiful, with a sparkling tip.

Amaya, Sakina, Sabino, and the teens gathered around as Star presented the glittering wand to Asha.

"Is that a magic wand?" Gabo asked, his eyes wide.

Asha held up her hands. "Thank you, but . . . no thank you," she told Star. "I'm no good with magic. I mean, I put a dress on a tree."

Gabo shrugged. "I'll take it," he said, reaching for the wand.

Star pulled the wand back just as Dahlia grabbed Gabo's collar. "Nope," Dahlia told him. "It's for Asha."

Star offered the wand to Asha once again, encouraging her to take it.

"But what am I supposed to do with it?" Asha asked.

Dario's face lit up. "Be our fairy godmother," he suggested.

"No, I couldn't be that," Asha said with a giggle.

But no one else was laughing. When she looked around at her friends' faces, she saw that they all loved the idea. Star gave an enthusiastic nod.

"I could?" she asked. She hesitantly reached out and took the wand.

Star waved, urging Asha to give the wand another try, so she did. Her friends dodged out of the path of the wayward magic, which landed on . . . Clara, the chicken perched on Safi's head. The hen grew in size until she was twice as large as Safi!

"Clara!" Safi exclaimed in wonder.

In all the excitement, Clara laid an egg—an egg so large that it knocked Gabo to the ground.

"Ah!" cried Gabo. "And you wonder why I'm grumpy."

"Sorry," said Asha, lowering the wand.

"Don't worry," Dahlia said gently. "Star will help you get the hang of it."

Asha grinned until she noticed the guilty expression on Star's face. "Oh no. I know you too well now," she said sadly. "You're going soon, aren't you? So you can be there for others to wish on." She gazed up at the spot in the sky where she'd first seen Star's twinkling light.

"Oh, I will miss you!" Valentino wailed. A heart-broken sob erupted from his throat. "My voice is really high when I cry," he admitted with a sniffle.

Star quickly crocheted a tiny handkerchief and handed it to him. Then Star looked up at Asha, as if to say it was her turn to comfort him.

Asha stepped forward and cupped the little goat's face in her hands. "Soon doesn't mean tonight, Valentino," she assured him, wiping away his tears.

"Oh, thank goodness," Valentino said, smiling through his sniffles. "That was too much for me. I'm only three weeks old after all!"

"How can we ever thank you, little Star?" Sabino asked.

Star locked eyes with Asha. They both smiled.

"That's easy," Asha replied. "Just keep wishing."

Star gave Asha a big hug and then zipped over Rosas, lighting up the early morning sky with glittering fireworks. With the wand in her hand and her family and friends by her side, Asha knew with certainty that now anything truly *was* possible in the Kingdom of Wishes.